The Emperor's Daughter

By Bill Morris

New ◯ Sun Publications

Half Moon Bay, California

Dedication

To Morris, Joan, Ruth, Dave, Grandma Cleo, Granddad Herald—loved ones present and past.

And, of course, to my loving family, who let me have this fantasy life.

Bill Morris

The Emperor's Daughter

Emperor's Quote

"I was a slave, but I chose you as my Master."

The Emperor

Prolog

On April 1st, 1984, the Free Royal Social Republican Bank of Denmark purchased a spanking brand new Infini-Checque machine from the Spinardi-Swiss National corporation.

Spinardi-Swiss specialized in providing money machinery to government mints. Spinardi-Swiss clients were among the largest and smallest countries the world over. If a small African nation wanted to print its money in grass huts on paper cut from brown paper bags, Spinardi-Swiss would help do it. Putting millions into research and development, Spinardi-Swiss would design and manufacture a brown-paper-bag money printer, and hand deliver the machine themselves (—all hoping that the little African country was still there by the time they arrived at the border.) Technicians would arrive to help install the machine in the hut.

The new Danish Infini-Checque was designed to put 75 bank note inspectors out of work. It was a massive 50-ton, computerized video camera that looked at the newly printed sheets of money as they came off the presses. It could scan up to six thousand sheets an hour for printing flaws. Bad bills were sprayed with black ink and sheets separated into a Good and a Bad pile. It required two technicians, one with brains and one without, to run it.

The Infini-Checque worked fantastically. It could tell a good bill from a bad bill because of an immense amount of programming. Six banks of parallel run computers allowed it to know what a good bill looked like. When the two camera eyes of the machine peered down on the fast moving rollers that dragged thousands of sheets by, the machine had enough programmed sense to see what was a good bill (within acceptable tolerances) and what was a bad one. And it spit black ink on the bad ones.

Denmark was going to save a lot of money by putting the 75 specially trained currency inspectors out of work and installing an Infini-Checque.

On April 12th, the Infini-Checque was put into service. The Danish money mint hummed.

Prolog Two

Two weeks later, the economy of Denmark collapsed.

Prolog Three

On January 1st, 1985, the Grand Central Democratic New Christian Left government of Belgium purchased and installed an Infini-Checque in the Belgian First National Mint.

Three days later, the Belgium economy collapsed.

Whoops!

Prolog Four

A rumor began to circulate internationally that someone called the Emperor, an incredibly bright new criminal mind, was at work.

Prolog Fini

Emperor's Comment:

So I made a few beginner mistakes. Big deal. It all depends on how you see it.

Chapter 1

I leaned out my second story window and shouted.

"Watch out!"

Looking down, I realized that Morgan's Eagle-Eye Detective Agency had struck again.

Leaning back from my desk, I had accidentally tapped the six-inch plastic pot of geraniums, blooming fiercely, with my elbow, knocking it off the window sill.

Again.

As I looked down, Abdul, my office slave, walked over to see the damage.

"Did you hit anyone?"

I grimaced.

Abdul took a cautious peek out the window himself.

Abdul blinked and said, "Man, he really looks angry."

I nodded.

"Good thing bicyclists wear those funny helmets," I said.

Abdul walked back to his desk where our paper work lay waiting. It was piled up around his rainbow-striped computer terminal. Abdul was busy painting it so himself.

"It is my rainbow tool of data gatherment," he said in his thick Indian accent as he stepped back, paintbrush in hand, admiring it. "A colorful window of my own personal empowerment, so to be speaking."

"Granted," I replied.

"Boss, your window has a way of rewarding people who happen under it," said Abdul to the air. Then he snickered.

I thought back two months to the cop who had walked under my detective agency window and been beaned with the flower pot. Another unfortunate gift from above. He'd been on the look out in our back alley for thievery and devious pursuits. My pot had hit him out of thin air.

Dirt on his shoulders and the bill of his hat, he'd pulled his gun and prepared to drill me as I stood aghast in the window.

"Officer! I didn't see you walking under my pot!" It was all I could think to say in a panic.

His first shot spanked the bricks hard beside my window.

Then I convinced him that I had surrendered, it was an accident, and he shouldn't shoot any extra taxpayers.

Abdul had crouched behind his desk, laughing at me the whole time.

Windows looking out on the world can turn out to be a lot of trouble.

Chapter 2

I run a one-man, one-slave, detective agency in downtown San Francisco. My name is Morgan Hercules. I'm the detective.

When the unfortunate window incident occurred, I was taking a break between jobs, cleaning up the paper work. I had just finished the Hamburger case.

It had been another case where somebody, a young twenty-year-old, was avoiding her Destiny and it came to get her.

By Destiny, I mean the name your mother and father put on you at birth. You know how people grow up to be in league with or against their names? Charles Spitz grows up to be Dr. C. Spitz, a great dentist. John Putter chops his way up from caddy to golf pro. Mary Anne Biggapples, a striptease artist.

You can embrace your Destiny or remake it.

I tend to favor those that try to remake it. I like the kind of knothead people who look out a window one day and say, I'm not going to be this person anymore. I'm going to change my name.

Like John Merryman, a Denver boy who came to San Francisco at seventeen. A hard worker, he became an international leader in the Homosexual Rights movement. He saw a lot of suffering and at twenty-one decided to fix it. Got up on stages with a megaphone. John Merryman changed his name to Ima Gaye. He did a good hula, too.

My last clients had been two parents who wanted me to find their missing 18-year-old daughter.

Of course, she was missing: her name was Kola N. Hamburger.

After about two weeks of searching I'd located Kola. She'd been walking the streets, and been pretty mistreated. She was now wearing a kind of hippie-garb, long fairy-like strings of wispy hair flying from her head. Rainbow colored jeans. An amulet that looked like blue ice hung between her nearly exposed breasts from an unbuttoned sweater.

She'd taken a new name: Milky Goodheart.

Of course, there's always room for one more Milky Goodheart on Haight street. Although this was a dietary upgrade, much lower in cholesterol than Kola N. Hamburger, the local ruffians had also begun abusing her. You know, abusers who had had mothers who always said sternly, "Now drink your milk, you little bastard!"

So Kola N. Hamburger was being smashed flat.

Her Destiny.

I talked her into going home to her parents. I told her Milky Goodheart was going a bit too far. She suggested maybe she should change her name to Black Mamba.

We settled on Casandra Lionheart.

So she went back to face her parents and get that name and a lot of other family stuff off her shoulders.

I hope she did.

My full name is Morgan Theodore Roosevelt Einstein Hercules.

My mother really piled it on.

Chapter 3

As head of the Morgan Eagle-eye Detective Agency, I work out of a little office in the one brick building for miles in San Francisco. I can see a wharf and a parking lot and bums from my window. My office is just about the size where two men can walk around without bumping shoulders. Abdul and I know each other well, so the office size isn't a problem. It has a calendar on the wall from 1985 that shows a picture of the *Goddess of Bikinis* so stunning I never changed months. Time stopped that day. We also have the standard filing cabinets, a computer terminal, and a door with clouded glass that visitors try to look through.

Our office has two windows, one for me and one for Abdul.

Watch out for the pot if you walk under mine.

Don't worry, if you consciously know it's there, I could never hit you.

It's the unknowing that tend to get knocked further unconscious.

Chapter 4

Years ago, my mother didn't want me to open a detective agency.

To be precise, she said, "Morgan, you can't even find your own socks."

Chapter 5

In spite of that, I am a decent detective. Been working at it for years. I'm also good at disguises. I learned the true secret for making a disguise work: look like yourself. Be just another person like yourself. Be a human.

We all kind of think wearing disguises is like dressing up in costumes and acting like something you're not. A kind of sneaky costume party. But it's not so. I've watched enough monster movies to learn otherwise.

In the movies, monsters spend most of their time on the screen as ordinary human beings. The werewolf works as a bearded plumber with torn pants, the vampire is a fashion model who looks deeply into the eye of the camera. Yes, inviting you to want her. True monsters walk around nonchalantly, unremarkably in human skins. They do this everyday all day.

But inside their human skins, they are monsters.

The sexual full moon rises, and unknowingly watched by his own young daughter, the bearded plumber turns into a wolf, rapes an eight-year-old playmate, slams her head with a rock, kills her and hides the corpse under a dirty mattress. The daughter has a tough time dealing with this. Should she turn in her father and end her life as she knows it? Or was it a dream, a horrible nightmare? Traumatized, daughter forgets everything, even her childhood, and later becomes an addict. And the bearded plumber back in human skin whistles while he repairs pipes.

The beautiful model vampire meets you alone in a hotel room, gets you panting with lust, and lets you have her. And then she bites your neck. Over a long slow period she visits you nightly, shedding her ordinary human form and becoming a glorious monster that secretly sucks out your emotional blood. You welcome her each visit, she is *ravishing*. But she never stays. After each session, you turn whiter, until you're nearly dead.

And then you are dead.

She leaves.

You look in the mirror and you don't see yourself. That's because you're dead, and now you're a vampire.

Now you have to walk around among the living pretending an ordinary life. Now you have to find a human disguise.

Some might object and say what about Frankenstein? Now there's a monster who barely looked human at all. Clumping around with shoulders as if he were wearing a horse-collar. Moaning and raising a clutched hand as he stumbled after people. That's not a monster in a human disguise.

Of course! Frankenstein is not a true monster. Just the opposite, he's a true human in a monster disguise. He's a man honestly trying to get beyond his own ugliness. He's doing the opposite of what monsters do. He's a human being wearing a monster suit.

And that's why they set his pants on fire.

Of course, after being a detective these many years, I know these monsters actually exist. It's just in the realm of the human spirit. And they never take off their human disguises when they do the damage.

Chapter 6

I am a few years past forty-five, but I look okay. I have a kind of leaner John-Wayne face and a square chin. Well, not quite square, but at least I have a chin. I mean I don't crack walnuts with my biceps or anything, but I can do a good number of sit-ups and pushups. I also have a temper that is monolithic. Although I rarely lose it, at the right stimulus, my temper can send me into a state that can only be characterized as *inspired*.

Once I was tracking down a drug dealer's twelve-year-old daughter who had been abducted by a rival gang of drugsters. This jittery dealer had come to me desperate to get back his daughter —

and fast, before his wife found out. He'd literally pushed dirty bundles of twenties into my hands telling me where the other gang hung out and where Priscella, his junior-high schooler, could be found.

Like the French say: *L'argent n'a pas d'odeur.* (Money don't stink.) But by looking at the grimy, flimsy, lint-ball covered bills, it really goes into foul places.

There was also a sense of urgency for me with this little girl involved. Priscella! What kind of name was that for a drug dealer's daughter?

I went down to this junky restaurant in the inner city, actually a tacqueria joint where this drug team pursued business.

As I entered I was surprised to see the gang was a group of quite young black 14- to 18-year-olds lounging like leopards on chairs and tables. There wasn't a scent of cooking or a taco in sight. I proceeded to hold court telling my audience that Priscella had disappeared. All heads turned my way like a compass needle of disdain.

One of the older meaner looking dudes looked at me with a snaky grin, fished something on a chain out from his shirt collar, and said, "Hey man, but she ain't totally disappeared."

On the chain was a human ear.

I pushed over a table and pulled off a leg. Then I lost my temper.

Even in my anger I was careful to hit the mushy parts of human bodies. I didn't hit skulls and splatter brains like burst water balloons against the walls. I did leave a good number of grapefruit-size bruises on wincing bodies. All were so terrified that no one pulled a pistol and shot me.

To my surprise, I found the injured girl later in a back storeroom. I took her to the local ER. I was still coming down from the big bowl of adrenaline soup I'd just had. As usual, I was a bit aghast with myself. Beating these young capitalists, who because of skin color were forced to work outside the law, and thus were doomed to an ugly downward spiral of lawlessness and violence, beating such characters was no badge of honor. (Sharp-minded practitioners of the marketing laws of supply and demand, within the law they might have had a company name like Scripts, instead of the Crips.) And I like to think of myself as a cool head. But that ear thing got me.

My vengeful temper, it is a strange feeling of anger and invincibility. I call it, "The Wrath of God."

Abdul, who has seen me in this state once or twice, calls it, "Making a hard first impression; and multiple hard impressions after that."

Chapter 7

Abdul Dalaah is my faithful office slave. Technically because I pay him and he is free to go, he is my trusty, ever-ready servant. And a whiz at getting me information off the computer. Actually he runs my office so well, scheduling appointments, calling in late payments, filtering bogus clients who really just want my sympathetic ear for an hour so I can tell them to forget it and go home, and just generally keeping me cracking as a business—well there are times I feel he's the wily master, me slave.

Although he's near sixty, he's surprisingly young at heart. In truth should he ever decide to take his cheery joker face elsewhere, I would be devastated. He has made himself indispensable. He knows it so he sticks with me. Besides, I do a lot of child recovery work, which he likes. It calls for much computerized searching and an occasional rescue call that he accompanies me on giggling like an amateur.

I don't know why he has the Muslim name Abdul. He's definitely Hindu. For the first week after I hired him he went around calling me *Sahib*.

Now I like a good ego stroke as much as any person, but in an American detective business, it doesn't make for the right image if you have a little brown man bowing and calling you *Sahib* as he brings you tea. (I might want to reinstall this behavior, however, should I start a brothel or white slave trade.)

Abdul once told me his mother runs an Indian restaurant called the *Emperor's Intrigue* in Edinburgh Scotland. He went so far as describing specific menu items, one of which was called *indescribables*.

"What are indescribables?" I asked.

"They are small pieces of onion cooked in greasy batter. They are served cold. Let me tell you, they are indescribable," Abdul said.

"Indescribable good?" I asked.

"No, indescribable bad, very bad."

Abdul smiled and shrugged.

"It's called the *Emperor's Intrigue* because the menu is full of inedible objects with mysterious names."

Chapter 8

Emperor's comment:

"It just so happens I have eaten at the *Emperor's Intrigue*. The food was indeed terrible, the *indescribables* like eating buttons. That Abdul, growing up eating there all the time as a kid, how did he survive it? He must have had an iron gizzard."

Chapter 9

I was having one of those harried days where all I can do is flap my hands around on my desk, searching for papers. Busy, worried, not finding anything. My desk is really a kind of traffic snarl. I 'm the kind of guy that might use a dab of jelly as a paper clip. I'm sure under the elbow high*lost pile*, the big one I never visit on the left, under there are crumbs and such that no rat can get. So by now you're wondering, how does that office make money? Of course, Abdul comes along and steals the really important top layer off the desk and fills out the forms, pays the bills, duns the late payers himself. He's the miracle desk scavenger.

What I'm good at I guess would be shooting a hole in it—if it should move.

I blew out my cheeks and let my lips do a horse buzz.

Abdul raised his head.

"Yeah, Boss?"

"Have you seen that late payment notice on my mortgage around here?"

"Yes, I found it last week, right next to the lottery ticket I bought you last month." He got up and snatched a sheaf from the file cabinet and walked it over to me.

He placed it in front of me like a plate before the starving.

"Thanks," I said, looking down studying the depressing document.

"Did we win? The lottery, I mean?" I asked as Abdul headed back to his desk.

Abdul shrugged as he sat down.

"Yes," He said matter-of-factly, adjusting himself before his computer terminal.

"You won $153,000 dollars. It was a 57-way split with the other winning ticket holders. I deposited the first check in your checking account last week."

Abdul looked at me and smiled a little bird-like smile.

I checked: the remainder of the overdue mortgage stated I owed $153,000 and two cents.

Abdul miracle worker!

The two cents I could come up with on my own.

Just then there was a meek knock on the office door. It was so meek, that it was almost a nudging on wood.

Grinning, I nodded for Abdul to get it.

I called, "Let the world in, we are ready for business."

Chapter 10

As Abdul got up, the person behind the door, not knowing she could be seen from our side, moved her face up and down against the office door's cloudy glass, trying to peer in. This looked like the head bobbing of an owl trying to look through an impossibly thick fog.

Abdul opened the door, nodded his head, smiled gravely, then said, "Come in, Julie."

As I watched with curiosity, a startling being walked into my view.

It was a look that Marilyn Monroe or Jane Mansfield would have died for. Her hair was the sheened and extreme blond of polished hay, clipped helmet-shaped with two curls that ran down her cheeks. Her oval face had shapely cheekbones, an exquisite soap-dish white complexion, and penetrating blue eyes. When I say penetrating, I mean the kind of blue eyes that can drive a nail through your thrilled heart. She had a high forehead and thoughtful eyebrows. She wore no make up. She had a mouth you wanted to drink from.

Her smile was an uncertain grimace as she advanced toward me. With a blue beret on her head at a raked angle, she wore a deep blue dress that, although it had an academic cut, still clung to her hips and other right places like a towel. She had a shapely feminine walk.

I realized I could now turn the calendar page on the *Goddess of Bikinis*.

The young woman stopped in front of my desk. Oddly, attached by a red ribbon on her lapel was what looked to be a monocle.

Indeed the woman picked up the lens and fixed it in her right eye like a jeweler's glass. Looking at me through the newly affixed facial accouterment, she now appeared as a cross between a school marmish librarian and a man-killing diva. With her uncertain air, she seemed somewhat mystified about who she was herself.

She put out her hand.

Speechless, I got up from my desk in a stoop and shook it.

Still standing in the doorway as if reluctant to come in himself,

Abdul said solemnly, "Boss, this is Julie Veingold."

Chapter 11

"Glad to meet you, Julie."

I waved my hand vaguely toward the chair behind her and she nodded and sat down.

I sat, smiled, then looked over with a raised eyebrow at Abdul.

"Boss, Julie needs some help, and I suggested that you might help her..." said Abdul.

"How do you know Abdul?" I asked of the young woman.

"Well, we live together in the same building." She smiled uncomfortably. Then she hastened to add, "Well, we don't live together, I mean I live in a different apartment and all, but it's the same building where Abdul is concierge, but really he's almost part of my family."

"Abdul, you're a concierge at Julie's apartment building?" I asked.

"Well, Boss, it's kind of like that. I 'm living in the same building, in the basement which is quite nice and roomy, and it's what I do, you know, at night, take care of things..." Abdul said, covering the surprise of his moonlighting.

Julie blustered in, "Well, really, Abdul is so much a part of my family, he's been in the building so long, and sometimes eats with us and all..." Somehow Julie was trying to help with covering Abdul's night work.

"Okay, okay," I said, raising my hand.

"Julie has a problem, Boss," said Abdul.

"Let's let Julie tell it," I suggested.

Julie nodded, her blue beret making a small bird peck.

"It's about my family. I need help finding someone. Abdul said maybe you could help me, but I can't pay a lot, but Abdul says that's not a problem, the way you run your office...oh!"

Julie pulled herself up short, hoping she hadn't insulted me by mentioning inside information about my office procedures.

"Abdul would know about that," I said kindly, taking no offense.

"It's a missing persons case, and a medical situation, Boss. You'll be understanding it," volunteered Abdul. He scrunched his mouth up in a supplicating grimace.

"I hope to," I said, then waited in silence for Julie to continue. A bright girl, she soon nodded and began again.

"Well, to start from the beginning, Mr. Hercules," said Julie.

"Morgan," I interrupted.

"Morgan, yes," nodded Julie smiling and continuing.

I sat back enjoying that this beautiful girl with a monocle had called me Morgan.

"I live with my family in Abdul's apartment building. Not really my family really, because my sister and I, well we're orphans, and we live with Aunty Dotty, our foster mother, caretaker really. You see my mother died when I was born, I never knew her. But Aunty Dotty told me she was a brilliant scholar, a Ph.D. in Linguistics from George Town University, but that's about all I know, I don't really have any pictures of her."

"And you want me to find her?" I asked.

"Well, no, she's dead," said Julie, a bit disconcerted.

"Sorry, I jumped ahead, thinking maybe you thought she was still alive..."

Julie looked at me a moment with suspicion as if I'd just had my brains vaccinated.

"Well, no, it's about my sister. You see...the doctor's report says she's quite sick. It's leukemia and if we don't find someone for a bone marrow transplant, she'll die..."

"Is this your younger sister?" I asked.

"No, she's about 17 years older than me. She's 42. I'm not the right type for a transplant, and so we have to find someone else in my family. This is my sister here."

Julie handed me an old photograph with a dog-eared corner. In it stood two girls, one indisputably Julie at about twelve, and next to her stood a broad smiling, slope-shouldered young woman. My eyebrows edged together as I looked at Julie's sister and realized that this round-faced woman with slightly Asian eyes definitely had Down syndrome. She was a half-grown child-woman, rather, smiling with incredible good-nature out on an uncomfortable world.

"Your sister, she's..." I hesitated.

"Down syndrome, yes, but she's—" Julie took a breath before diving in. I jumped in first.

"Julie, I'm sorry to ask this, but don't Down syndrome folks, don't they have shortened life expectancies? Your sister..."

"Anna Elisabeth," Julie added.

"Yes, Anna Elisabeth, you said she's 42 already. Isn't that..."

"Unusual?" volunteered Julie, "No, well maybe, but she's been doing so well. It's just lately she's been sick. Then the doctor came back with this terrible report and all."

I had to ask it. "Do you think anyone will be offering a bone marrow transplant to a middle-aged Down syndrome person?"

Julie sat up abruptly with dignity.

"Yes, I would, if I had the marrow."

I believed she would.

I nodded, impressed.

"She's my sister. She doesn't have a mother, all she has is me. If I don't try to find a donor...well, she doesn't have anyone else to fight for her. I have to." Julie was staring at me with accusing eyes, as if I'd suggested abandoning her sister, which I had, I guess.

"So Julie is wanting you to be finding a relative of her's," added Abdul.

"What about your father?" I asked.

"I never knew anything about him. I don't have any pictures at all of my mother or father. Only pictures of my sister and I, and of course, Aunty Dotty."

"What happened to your father?" I asked.

Julie raised perplexed shoulders then dropped them like heavy weights.

She opened her purse and took out an orange sheaf of paper. She handed the paper to me to open and read.

"I never knew anything about my father. Not until just this week, when this paper was shoved under my door. Right at the time when I was most desperate to find someone to help my sister. Then one morning Anna found this, and brought it to me."

I opened the sheaf of paper. It read:

Your Father is the Emperor.

I looked up.

"We have to find him," Julie said.

Chapter 12

"And who is the Emperor?" I asked, looking at Abdul as if he were the only person who could really tell me.

My Indian wizard computer researcher only looked back at me gravely. I could see him carefully considering his words.

Whenever Abdul begins considering before he speaks, I begin preparing for the worst.

"Oh, Boss, he's an immensely powerful guy. Boss, he's the big Kahuna of the underworld, the Capi di tutti capi, the head shark, the Grand Kabob, the Cannibal Chief, the meanest gator in the swamp..." Abdul was waxing poetic.

"He may be my Dad," broke in Julie quietly.

Abdul hesitated.

"Yes, maybe, Julie, sorry. Sorry." Abdul made three quick apologetic bows from the waist.

"Could we be a little more specific?" I asked.

Abdul straightened from his supplications and addressed me again.

"It is only rumors, but the rumors are many. The Emperor is a master-mind controlling many many things. Many things criminal, many things not so criminal. It is said he is being a master to many many endeavors. Remember years back when Denmark got into trouble, and the whole country went broke, inflation hit so hard, the Danish kids pushed around wheelbarrows of cash to buy ice cream cones? Well, they say the Emperor was behind it, somehow. And it happened in Belgium, too. It is said he is so powerful because he is practically made of money. He has more money than the baboon has fleas, he has more money than sand on all the beaches. And if you walk away with any of his sand between your toes..."

"Spare me the metaphors, please Abdul," I pleaded.

"Right, Boss," said Abdul.

"So this guy, the Emperor, controls the Mafia?" I asked.

"Oh, bigger, bigger than the Mafia. The Mafia, they are afraid of him. He is The Master of all the masters."

I grimaced and looked over to see how Julie was taking all this. She'd indeed grown more slump-shouldered as Abdul went on.

"You sure you want to find him?" I asked Julie.

"I have to," was her meek reply, "Anna Elisabeth..." She shrugged to complete her sentence.

Let's see, I was about to go looking for the biggest criminal on earth to see if he would be a donor to a Down syndrome woman-child.

"Will you help me? Find out if he is my father?" asked Julie.

I looked at her beauty.

"Sure, no problem," I said.

Chapter 13

I asked a few more questions about whether they had got a second medical opinion of Anna Elisabeth's condition. Abdul said he had. Julie nodded. I said I'd have to think about how to go about finding the Emperor, I couldn't very well just lean out my window and call his name, hoping to clunk him on the head with my flower pot. Abdul and I would confer about tactics. I told Julie that I'd best start by visiting her home, talking to Aunty Dotty, and generally snooping into her past. Again Julie nodded all was okay with her. I set up to come and visit her at her apartment that evening.

Abdul said that he'd take me there.

Julie left with another handshake and meek nod of the blue beret. I watched that walk all the way out the door.

After Abdul closed the door behind her, he turned to me and said, "Thanks, Boss, she's needing someone to help her."

"Trouble is," I said, "I ain't the meanest gator in the swamp."

Abdul grinned.

"Good one, Boss."

Chapter 14

I conferred with Abdul about our initial strategy. It was decided he would do the usual background checks on Julie's family and a broad computer scan of data for information relating to the so-called Emperor.

"I'll have all that for you in a snappy," said Abdul, resolutely. I could tell he was happy to be on the hunt, sniffing out data trails.

"Well, it seems this guy the Emperor drips with money. Money flows. Get me also a list of known associates, anyone that his money might flow to...Dig up everything you can. Somebody contacted Julie about the Emperor here in San Francisco, so somebody knows about him here. While you do the searches, I'm going out to make a contact, see if anything turns up locally."

"Right," said Abdul.

"So snappy to it," I said, and headed for the door.

Chapter 15

While Abdul did his computer search, I thought I'd do the first thing I always do when checking out a missing person: check the underworld.

You go down into that underworld, you always find a lot of missing things. Like neglect, spurious religious beliefs, and dirty socks, a lot of these things you didn't really want to find. But there the underworld had them, waiting for you under your bed.

I got in my car and headed down to a contract muscle-man I knew. He was a retired boxer, but he occasionally came out of retirement to perform his old job again, but this time on unsuspecting people. This made the job easier, he said.

His real name was Joe Lewis, but this wasn't flashy enough, so at the beginning of his career, he'd changed it to Sugar Ray Mohamed Ali.

Sugar had done well for a while and even fought a championship fight, but lost it when walking back to his corner after a round, he tripped and fell, hit his head on the ring post, and knocked himself out.

I pulled up to his little suburban cottage with its neatly clipped lawn and geometrically parallel knee-high clipped hedge. Sugar's wife worked, while Sugar stayed home and took care of the kid. So Sugar got down and developed some very refined yard and housekeeping skills.

I walked up the steps to the front door. The door was open and all that kept me from walking right in was a screen door. I peeked in to see Daniel, a small boy about four, Sugar's son, sitting with his nose to the TV clutching a bit inflated toy. It was an inflated hammer, about three feet long with a handle as thick as a salami, the kind a kid wins at a carnival.

"Hammer! Hammer!" shouted Daniel at the TV. Then he gave it several slamming bops with his tool.

I tapped a knuckle on the door.

"Sugar?" I called in.

I heard the heavy footsteps of the monster approaching. I know that sounds like something out of Frankenstein, but it's true. Sugar Ray Mohamed Ali was a big guy, huge shoulders and pumpkin-size hands. He lumbered side to side as he walked.

He squinted out through the screen at me.

"Hey, Sugar, how's it going?" I called in.

Sugar nodded once, looked at me without expression. That was the signal for me to get out my wallet.

I took out fifty dollars.

"I need some information," I said, waving my money like a little flag between my fingers.

"General or specifics?" asked Sugar, noncommittally.

"General," I said.

Sugar shrugged. "Come on in."

"Hammer!" yelled Daniel as he excitedly bopped the TV top a good one.

I consciously wiped my feet and stepped in.

Sugar's living room was immaculately kept, sofa plush and white, perfectly aligned, potted plants perky and fresh, and spotless windows.

I looked around the place and nodded my approval. Sugar smiled and shrugged again.

"Daniel, how you doin? Pretty Good?" I asked.

Daniel turned and looked at me and his face scrubbed up into a smile, "Hammer!"

Sugar shook his head ruefully, "Seems like all Daniel says now is hammer. This week it means 'yes'."

"When she was pregnant, his mother must have been frightened by a nail," I said.

Sugar Ray Mohamed Ali smiled and nodded, but didn't get it.

"Yeah, sure that happens a lot," was his reply.

I nodded. Daniel turned back to his TV.

"Sugar, you know anything about the Emperor?"

As I looked, the welcome in Sugar Ray Mohamed Ali's big face retracted a bit.

"You mean the guy that did that Denmark thing?"

"Yeah," I said. "You ever heard anything?"

Sugar put out his frying pan size hand and I put the fifty dollars in it like a fish. But it didn't sizzle.

"Well," said Sugar, "I really don't know much about the Emperor. Except he's a pretty powerful dude. I don't know if I'd mess with him. I did a job for him once. But I didn't talk or learn nothing about him."

"What kind of job?"

Sugar looked over at Daniel and called, "Hey, you want a cookie?"

Daniel looked over at his dad.

"Hammer!"

"Whyn'tcha go out in the kitchen and get one then..." said Sugar.

Without a word Daniel got up and left the room, lugging his big inflatable hammer like a pickax on his shoulder.

"He takes after his Dad," I said.

Sugar smiled pleased.

"You did a job for the Emperor? What kind of job?" I asked.

"Somebody called me and said the Emperor wanted somebody messed up. This somebody had messed up one of the Emperor's people, so I was to beat this guy up in return."

"Who did you work on?" I asked.

Sugar made kind of a sheepish ducking motion with his head.

"My older brother," admitted Sugar.

"Sugar Ray Cassias Clay?" I said.

"Yeah," said Sugar.

"You took a contract to mess up your own brother?"

"Hey, when you're in the hitting business, you're in the business. You can't say no. It's suspicious, you know?"

"They lines the opponents up and you knocks them down," I said.

"Something like that," Sugar said with a rueful nod. Then he brightened a bit, "Besides, I was the perfect guy for the job. I know my brother has this sore left shoulder...so all I had to do was circle left..." Sugar went into a pugilist's hunting crouch, his two hands up like gunsights.

As I tried to smile without wincing, Daniel walked back into the room carrying two cookies.

"You have any contact with the Emperor?" I asked.

Sugar said no, that the next day a little brown man had walked up to his door and given him an envelop with the money.

"That's all I know," said Sugar.

Daniel walked up and held out a cookie to me.

"Well, thanks," I said, "Are they good?"

"Hammer," said Daniel shyly.

He was the cutest curly-haired little black kid. I took the cookie and gave it a nibble. Then I gave it a big munch and chewed energetically.

"Like it?" asked Daniel.

"Hammer," I said.

Daniel laughed.

I said my thank you's to both Sugar and Daniel and left.

I realized for my money all I'd learned was that the Emperor used a little brown man as a runner just like me.

Chapter 16

Yes, I wade in and muck around in the criminal world. I play carefully and try not to get dirty. I don't find it so dangerous or hard to understand. I mean their underhanded, out-law ways of making money are pretty arcane, as devious and probably hurtful as the human mind can devise.

But I mean what are criminals working for?

Money, self-esteem, security, leisure-time, a better life.

Maybe we should just give it to them.

I basically see two types of criminal: those working for cash, and those working for revenge.

Those working for cash usually are the disenfranchised underclass who work as individual burglars or bandidos or band together in the old "it's better with an army" mentality and put the assault on the law abiding. Jimmy the doors of the rich. Clank the head of the unsuspecting until a wallet drops like black fruit from a forbidden tree. The targets should be the Haves with their flowering hedges and walls with electronic gates, which nowadays are more elegant than killer dogs and moats. But usually the targets are the ever-poor.

The criminals working for revenge, well, they're the worst. The abundantly abused crowds of teens and young who grow up with a low orange fire of hate in their eyes. Abandoned, neglected, beaten, confused. The receivers of hurt who just have to stop receiving. Till the small orange flames light in the backs of their eyes, and they start awaiting victims. You don't want to see that fire coming at you when you're alone in a dark alley.

Those working for revenge may disguise themselves as those working for cash. And they can become the most successful, heinous, and destructive. They are the kind that will shoot you for an Oreo. Or blast you in the groin because you didn't hand over the $50 in the till at the local 7-11 quite fast enough. Just a mean parting statement.

If the cure for the poor is more, what's the cure for the abused?

Brutal therapy in a cage?

Smash their faces in the shit until they quit seeing revenge and see a better life?

I don't know.

Chapter 17

Emperor's comment:

Well, Morgan the Criminal Seer is half right, I suppose. The criminal element is blind, but also very generous. When they stick you up or lunge with a hammer to harm you, you are a victim because they don't see you. They see only their own poverty, or vast amounts of abuse and their abuser before them. They don't see you. And they are just generously sharing with you their lives, blindly giving you what they have in their world. Ah, the generosity, the abundance, it's wonderful!

Chapter 18

I returned to the office to find Abdul standing at the laser printer chugging out report pages. Whereas I expected to find sheaves and sheaves of background material about Julie and the Emperor, only two little pages had churned out of the printer.

Abdul handed me the two sheets. One was a copy of Julie's birth certificate. The other was a list of a half dozen names.

"This is it?" I said to Abdul.

Abdul shrugged, "Unless you want Julie's report cards from elementary school through college, in which she received straight A's, excepting one C plus in Advanced Bowling. I didn't see much reason to bog us down with that."

"Adoption papers?" I asked.

"In accessible," said Abdul.

I looked over the print out of Julie's birth certificate. Born in 1970, which made her 25 years old. I checked the blanks for Father and Mother's name: the Mother's blank held only the name Veingold. The Née blank was left unfilled. I glanced at the Father's name: that blank held a "UA." which I assumed meant unavailable. The attending physician's name, Dr. Pushkin, was typed at the bottom, with a scrawl that the computer copy had darkened to make unreadable.

"Not much here," I said glumly to Abdul.

I switched to the second sheet. It was a short report and a list of potential associates of the Emperor.

"Why just this list?" I asked.

"There were only a few lines here and there on the Emperor, Boss. I found nothing in the newspaper archives that I can search. Nothing in the criminal records that I have access to. Only one file which mentioned the Emperor. It talks a bit about him, and lists suspected contacts."

"Where's the file from?" I asked.

"FBI, Boss."

"You broke into the FBI computer files?" My eyebrows were up in worried arches.

"Yeah, I did it again, Boss."

I heaved a sigh. Abdul had secret channels of information around the globe. Unfortunately, he would also pull the roots of his information from some of the most powerful, secretive, and vengeful offices the world over. The FBI computers were challenging haunts for a person of Abdul's computer wiles. It was also like juggling rattlesnakes. Once the FBI had raided the office next door, narrowly missing us by one address digit.

I read the FBI report:


```
Field Report 1002.67 -12/21/95

Agent Peter Gunlug, Grade 7 Eleventh Computer
Research Unit

Preliminary Background Report: Emperor

Top Secret: Class 10


July 8th, 1995, this office received a phone call
from one "Willie the Sneak" offering information
```

about a new criminal mind, now residing in the United States, in return for payment of $50,000 dollars. The informant told us that the information concerned a criminal master-mind named the Emperor. This person was said to be a manipulator of vast sums of money, and involved in some way with the economic collapse of several small, unimportant European countries, namely Denmark and Belgium.

Although the Bureau has no significant interest in Denmark or Belgium, a meeting was set up to discuss the facts pertaining to a European-based criminal setting up camp within our borders. A $1,000 check was authorized as payment to the informant, and I met with "Willie the Sneak" once on 07/05/95.

The informant produced as evidence a crumpled page that was a hastily scribbled on back of a bank slip, a transfer slip from a Swiss bank in Geneva. The informant said that he had stolen this slip from a trash bin at great risk to himself. On the slip, without identification numbers, was written in handwriting:

Emperor's list: US transfer 1987

Money to:

Bill Tubbman

John Achmyer

Mother Teresa

Grand High Wizard Joseph Hateplum KKK

Sergeant Conrad Voznesensky, US Marines

Dr. Billy Kookie

Dr. Theodore Needler

Charles Ashe

After questioning the suspect, I estimated the informant as an inane fool interested only in swindling money from the FBI (making him a true fool!) I canceled payment on the $1,000 check that afternoon.

Respectfully submitted,

Peter Gunlug

Eleventh Computer Research Unit

I looked up from reading the list of suspected associates.

"Mother Teresa?" I said aloud. "Am I supposed to believe this?"

Abdul shrugged and gave me his usual encouraging counsel, "It's reality, Boss. It's better than any fiction."

Chapter 19

About six that evening I went over to Julie's apartment. I'd followed the handwritten directions given me by Abdul. It was a large stone building in a better downtown residential section of the city, well-kept apartments that looked with expensive views out over the bay. I walked up the cement steps and pulled open the glass door.

I glanced around the lobby where spiral stairs wound up out of sight. An elevator framed in wood stood with resolutely closed door. Near the entry way was another door, firmly closed, that looked a bit like a maintenance closet with a large sign beside it in shiny brass letters.

Abdul Dallah, Concierge Extraordinaire.

I stood a second taking in the sign that had my office slave's name on it. I guess if you had a job title it doesn't hurt to put *extraordinaire* behind it.

It was strange that I'd worked with Abdul for years and didn't know he lived here, or was an off-hours concierge.

I rapped a knuckle on the door and waited.

"Boss! Good to see you. Ready to be seeing Julie?" cried Abdul as the door swung open, framing my small office mate.

I looked behind him to see reassuringly that a clean beige couch and shiny bookshelf filled with hardback books lounged behind him. At least my office slave wasn't living in penury. I'd secretly worried that I'd see an old sofa with the stuffing hanging out. I was relieved to see middle-class furnishings.

"Yes, which apartment is she in?" I asked.

"She's on the third floor, garden view. Five rooms, one and a half baths, one of our largest," replied Abdul, "though they've been having trouble with the garbage disposal lately. Anna Elisabeth keeps throwing Hershey bar tinfoil in, and it clogs the works."

"And that's your department, unclogging the works?" I said.

"Oh, yes, Boss. I'm an A-1 unclogger." Abdul smiled with a self-depreciating nod. "You just have to be having the right tools."

I nodded.

"Shall we be going up?" asked Abdul with a gesture toward the stairs.

"In a second," I said. "Tell me a bit more about Julie and her family. How long have you known them?"

"Oh, well, I've known Julie since she was just a kiddy. They are moving into this apartment when I did. Julie grew up here, and went to school here, and got her Ph.D. here. Stanford. She's a good girl."

"Does Julie have a job?"

"She teaches several courses, but really she's been completing her Ph.D. for that last several years. It's very hard, such studies. Her's is a new field, ground breaking, the field of psychological archaeology."

"And her sister? How, ah, bad is she?" I said.

"Meaning, Boss?"

"Can she use a paper clip, tie shoes, flip a pancake, read Faust, what?" I said.

"She's flipping pancakes but not reading Faust," said Abdul. "She's about a bright five-year-old mentally."

"Would it be a mistake to ask her questions?" I said.

"Yes, Boss," said Abdul.

I nodded.

"And the other one, this Aunty Dotty? What's she like?"

"Oh, I don't know if you'll be getting much from her. She's a feisty old closed-mouthed one. She is Indian like me, Boss. But she must have a shining heart: she adopted these two sisters. Both of them."

"But we don't have any information on that adoption?"

Abdul shook his head.

"Okay, let's go up," I said.

Abdul stretched out an arm as if pointing a pistol at the stairs, and said, "Follow me!"

Chapter 20

"Abdul! Good, you came, too," said Julie graciously as she opened the door to the apartment. Julie was wearing a black blouse with a thin pearl choker at her collar and a close-cut black skirt. The pink choker made her look prim as a jewelry store display.

"Nice of you to come, too, Mr. Morgan," Julie finished with a solemn business-like nod to me. She was toying with something with a red ribbon in her hands; it was her monocle.

"Just Morgan," I said.

"Oh yes, sorry. Please come in." Julie stepped back and Abdul and I entered a small hallway that led to a large living room.

The room was filled with books. Huge ceiling-high bookshelves surrounded the walls, mostly filled with thickish tomes, but with the occasional decorative vase or art piece that kept the room from being a library. There were two large plum-colored sofas, and in a corner a false-fireplace with an electric button on the wall beside it. I'd seen the kind: you press the button and the fireplace bursts in to gas flames. You press the button again and it goes out. On a small end table squatted a TV the size of a toaster and several slick magazines, Time, Newsweek, Vanity Fair. The room had several hallways leading away to unseen rooms.

Then I noticed an alcove where hung a overly-large portrait of a queenly seated woman. She was dressed in a blue ball gown with pink sash at her waist, hands cupped in her lap casually. The woman appeared young but self-assured. Her face had a high forehead with calm penetrating blue eyes that held a regal gaze beyond us. Surprisingly, a blue-jeweled tiara sat primly on her head. It was painted in stark oils with exquisite firm-handed technique, such that the sapphires of the tiara seemed to actually shine. The frame, like a great window looking into the room, was the heavy wooden kind you might see in a museum, guilded in false gold.

Julie caught me looking at the painting.

With a step toward the work she raised a hand with unconscious pride saying, "Do you like it, Morgan? That was my mother."

I nodded. "It's a fine work," I said.

"I don't know, of course. My mother died during my birth. But I've always believed I take after her," said Julie.

Julie turned and smiled not at me, but at the painting. I looked again at the stately woman elegantly posed with her tiara, in ballroom fantasy dress, and saw she was holding something odd in her hand. I looked closer: a monocle.

Chapter 21

"Thought you said you didn't have any pictures of your mother?" I asked.

"Please sit down," nodded Julie to the plum sofa near me. "That's right, this portrait is all I have. My mother, as I mentioned was a linguist, a Ph.D. at George Town University, when she died. I guess the portrait was done to honor her in some way. I don't have any other pictures. I didn't know anything about her, until I was four. I was kind of a lonely child, orphaned here with only Aunty Dotty and Anna Elisabeth. Actually, I was kind of pining away. Many little illnesses. The doctors said I was not thriving. Then one day, this huge package arrived. Aunty Dotty told me it was from a university where my mother had been. We opened this package and it was this portrait. You have to imagine, a young girl seeing her mother for the first time. It was an amazing vision, a wonder. And a very happy day in what had been considerable loneliness."

Julie laughed, "I remember dancing around the couch like a munchkin. Suddenly I was somebody. The daughter of a beautiful queen who was very smart. Silly, huh?" said Julie shyly. She affixed her monocle in her eye and squinted at me with a hesitant smile.

"Nearly like a fairy tale. But it meant a lot to you, I'm sure," I said.

Julie nodded without a word.

"You know nothing else about your mother?" I asked.

"No. I looked into it when I was older. There was a research paper or two listed in the Georgetown archives; I found them listed by computer, but there was no sign of the actual works when I went to retrieve copies. No personal effects either, Aunty Dotty told me something about a fire. No one seemed to remember her."

"How did you come to be with this Aunty Dotty?" I asked.

"I've just been with her from my first memories. She told me I was adopted when I was quite young. You see, I had blond hair, and Aunty Dotty is Indian with black hair. And Anna Elisabeth is blond, too. So I asked questions. And was told the little I know."

"No mention of your father, ever?" I asked.

Julie shook her head. "I didn't even know you had to have a man involved until I was 12. Just some kids had fathers and some didn't. And well, we kind of had Abdul, he was always coming over and taking us to the parks and zoos and even restaurants and such," Julie looked with a kindly glance at Abdul who was seated beside me on the couch.

Abdul raised his hand in a brief modest wave as I looked over at him.

"Can I talk with Aunty Dotty, to find out a bit more of your adoption?" I asked.

Julie shrugged. "You can try. But Aunty Dotty is getting a bit old, and well, stubborn."

Chapter 22

Julie rose and bid Abdul and I accompany her down a short hallway. We stopped before a cleanly painted door, and Julie tilted her head to it and knocked gently.

"Aunty Dotty? Are you awake? I have someone here to see you."

"Is it that bastard detective you were talking about who'll be snooping into our lives?" came an aged, wavering shout from the other side.

"Yes, Aunty Dotty," said Julie, with an embarrassed glance at me, "It's the one who'll be looking for my father."

"Tell him to kindly bug off."

Julie opened the door a crack and put her head through, "Aunty Dotty, he just wants to talk with you!"

"I adopted you. That's all. No one's looking into it so they can take my family away from me. Tell him to go suck hind tit!"

I glanced through the door. There sat an dark-skinned dowager with combed grey hair, a ring in her nose, a red dot on her forehead, and the eyes of an angry owl. The ancient woman was dressed in a long purple sari marked with shiny gold crescent moons and stars. She was seated like a priestess at a little coffee table, a jeweled wand of some sort in one hand, and a row of cards laid out solitaire fashion before her.

"Mrs. Dotty, may I speak with you?" I spoke through the doorway. The old woman calmly laid a black card down on the table and replied without looking up.

"Tell that snoopy dick head to stay away from me," said the old crone.

Julie looked my way apologetically. "She's telling fortunes and doesn't like to be disturbed."

I looked at Abdul and nodded in the crone's direction. "Maybe you could talk to her a bit. As a friend of the family?" I suggested.

"Sure, Boss," said Abdul and he cautiously walked in through the door.

Julie ushered me back down the hallway toward the living room.

"She's a feisty old lady," I said.

"She had a son once, a retarded boy she told me, but he died young. I suppose that's why she was willing to take in Anna Elisabeth and me. But now she believes strangers are often the bearers of bad news."

"I mainly take care of her and Anna Elisabeth now," said Julie with a meek smile.

Chapter 23

"Let's go to my study where we can talk," said Julie.

We had just turned down a short hallway toward an open office door, when I heard a thump to my left.

Looking over I saw a cleaning woman leaning over a large wicker basket piled with the escaping arms and legs of empty clothes. With her back to me, the woman was short and round-shouldered, and she bent taking a great armload of the wash and began stuffing the unmanageable pile into the open mouth of a washing machine. She leaned over the machine to stuff it in with her whole weight.

"Anna?"

The woman unstooped and turned with a smile to Julie and I. The woman I'd taken at first as a maid was unmistakably Julie's Down Syndrome sister. Anna, round-faced like a basketball, turned and gave an immense grin.

"Baby?" said the round-faced woman.

Julie glanced at me, explaining, "She calls me Baby. I'm her baby sister."

"Say hello to Mr. Morgan," called Julie.

Anna waddled toward me and extended a hand. Her eyes were bright and clear, and though her complexion was peaked, with lines of fatigue around the jowls and eyes, it was a look of innocent beaming welcome.

"Meetcha," said Anna. Anna and I shook hands in a few jerky bumps.

I said, "Glad to meet you, too, Anna."

The woman, through 42, stood smiling at me.

"I'm washing laundry," said Anna.

"Yes, I see," I said.

"Anna loves washing the clothes for us. She does a great job. We rarely have a stitch of dirty clothing around here. Do we, Anna?" said Julie.

Anna moved from foot to foot, ever smiling, and nodded enthusiastically.

"Can I wash your clothes?" Anna asked me.

Now this was hospitality.

"Not right now, Anna. I have them on. But maybe I'll come back on Sunday."

Julie laughed, and then Anna followed suit.

"This way," said Julie, indicating her office once again.

"Glad to meet you, Anna," I said as we left.

Like a bear, Anna waved a paw-like hand, turned and lumbered back to the washing machines. She opened a dryer door and began pulling out clothes like innards of a great cloth-eating animal.

"She doesn't look so sick," I remarked to Julie as we went into her office.

"No, the report says the Leukemia is in temporary remission. But the long-term prognosis is extremely poor. So we must act now."

"Does Anna go to school or anything?"

Julie shook her head, "She finished all that years ago. She's gone as far as she can. She loves doing housework and watching TV. She barely reads. I read to her some. We go for walks and such. She has no friends. It's a small world here. Anna's world.

"And your world?" I said.

Julie looked over her svelte shoulder at me, but didn't respond.

Chapter 24

As we entered Julie's office, I first saw packed bookshelves, then manila folders and an assortment of papers around a computer on a cluttered desk. It was a fairly standard academic office, a few comfortable chairs with collapsed stuffing and cushions. The faces of Jung, Freud, and various philosophers peaked from the jackets of books piled on desktop and floor. Dull colored clay masks and artifacts hung on walls, and several feathered poles stood in one corner. Small bones, beads, and broken pottery shards in several shoe boxes sat in another corner like a fleet of miniature boats. I turned around again to find a mahogany brown human skull seated atop Julie's computer monitor. It grinned at me with yellowed teeth.

"That's the skull of Ex-President Reagan," said Julie straight-faced to me, "He didn't need it."

"I guess Nancy was just bored with kicking the old thing around," I replied.

Julie laughed.

I enjoyed the sight.

Chapter 25

"Excuse the mess, I've only finished my dissertation just recently," said Julie seating herself at her desk.

I sat on the arm of a stuffed chair.

"Just exactly what is psychological archeology?" I asked.

"It's the study of myths and inherited psychological structures," said Julie. She smiled at me showing she was trying to be helpful. I could see she had the impression that she was talking to a pretty dinse bucket.

"You mean like Paul Bunyan and such?"

Julie looked around her at the crowds of her books and studies on the shelves as if expecting to see them shudder.

"Yes, it's a recent academic development."

"I did always think Paul Bunyan had secret subliminal needs long denied represented by Babe, his big blue Ox. Then maybe Babe was blue because she was just cold," I said.

"The old making love to Eskimos in the snow theory, huh?" said Julie with the slightest arch of an eyebrow signaling complete sarcasm.

"Children's stories," I said with a shrug.

"Which is no big deal unless you're living one. Pinning on a dishtowel and jumping down stairs is kind of a cute imitation of Superman. But not if you're still doing it at thirty-five. Subliminally, I mean," corrected Julie.

"I always look before I leap," I said. "And I'm told the salmon always swim subliminally up river every year."

"I certainly wouldn't want a salmon for a husband," snorted Julie, "Not flopping around in my bed."

"I check my bed before I get in. I don't know if that's archeological or psychological."

"Both, I bet," said Julie.

"Maybe," I laughed.

I looked at Julie. How the hell had we gotten onto talking about salmon going upstream and bed?

"Well, you're getting a false impression of psychological archeology. The premise is that you can live your whole life acting out inherited psychological structures—cultural messages, myths, stereotypes, and most importantly family values. Inherited psychological structures passed down from generation to generation. Some innocuous others harmful."

"Like if you got spanked, you'll spank your kids," I said.

"Yes," said Julie with a surprisingly charming tilt of her head encouraging with appreciation my little nugget.

"On a broader level, it poses questions about why one country develops the Hitler Youth and another the Boy Scouts. And it poses the question what's the difference?" Julie looked at the ceiling, flicking a sprig of blond hair from her eye.

"And what's the difference?" I asked.

"In certain terms, it can mean lives lost. Wars, inevitable accidents, alcoholism, addictions, and, of course, the loss of spiritual growth. People acting out roles that don't fit the present times or personality. People living out not just archetypal myths, like the myth of the heroic Paul Bunyan, that can drive the stake of heart attacks through the laboring hearts of loggers as it literally deforests the coasts, but also the acting out of the present day myths. Unconsciously looking up to societal personality types like Einstein, Teddy Roosevelt, even Hercules are modern day burdens the American man still carries around on his back. Psychological archaeology is about how we take on roles and visions, their meaning, and their eventual rewards or punishments."

I nodded. She'd actually mentioned my two middle names.

And last name.

"Like destiny," I said.

Julie laughed, "Now there's an age-old magical formula that can make people even give up their lives."

"I never minded watching Hercules on TV as a kid, watching those big Styrofoam rocks bounce off his head and chest. What's the harm there?" I poked in quizzically.

"Oh no great harm, of course, unless Hercules is actually invulnerable not only to rocks, but also to all his feelings, pain, anger, caring, sorrow, love...not unless *those* big boulders just bounce off him, too."

I shrugged, "Sometimes, in my world, the things I see, that might be better."

"My last name is Hercules," I grimaced in admission.

"Well, so it is," chuckled Julie, her cheeks deeply dimpled with an impertinent grin. "Excuse me if I picked an example that embarrassed you."

I shook my head brushing it off.

"Sorry," said Julie. Her blue eyes were merry, and I could see she was somehow inwardly amused at my expense. The amusement of P.H. Ds before the dwarfy intellects of the masses.

"The trouble with Hercules is that you're not sure whether he's a human or god. I think if you lose the human, you're in big trouble. Look at countries that act out their internal laws while exterminating lesser populations. All in the name of some Herculean concept of rightness and good."

"Yes," I said, "but when my clan descends on the criminals with machetes, it can also be a lot of fun."

Julie squinted her beautiful eyes at me before she abruptly howled with laughter.

Chapter 26

Abdul entered the room and smiling said, "You two seem to be getting along most becomingly."

"Yes, but the question is becoming what," I said dryly. Julie was dabbing her little fingers in the corner of her eyes. I didn't really mind being laughed at by a beautiful smart woman.

"Friends, colleagues, and allies, I'm hoping," replied Abdul.

"I'd settle for a TV sitcom," I said.

Julie smiled but didn't laugh.

Chapter 27

"Did Aunty Dotty have anything to tell you?" I asked of Abdul.

Abdul shrugged, "Only that you are a fool and I'm camels' unmentionables."

"Good news for modern man," I said, folding my hands in my lap.

"If Anna Elisabeth is sick why doesn't she want to help?" I wondered aloud.

"She doesn't believe Anna is sick, she says it's not in the cards, that poking around will bring death and harm," said Julie.

"She said that?" I said.

"Yes," replied Julie, "Then she said something strange. She shrugged and said, 'But then go ahead, every fool has to do it. Eventually the sun and moon come out.'"

"What does that mean?" I said.

"Don't look at me," shrugged Abdul, "I'm just camels' unmentionables."

Chapter 28

"So what is our first step in finding the Emperor?" asked Julie.

"Well, we've located a list of suspected associates. Abdul here pulled it from an FBI database."

"Who's first on the list?" asked Julie.

"Bill Tubbman," I said.

"The software billionaire?" said Julie.

"That's the guy," I said.

"How are you ever going to get in to see him? He must be surrounded by a dozen flunkies whose whole jobs are to keep people back," said Julie.

I smiled, taking my turn to look on Julie as someone who didn't have all the answers.

"Never underestimate the power of an Abdul," I said, pointing a thumb backhand at my office slave.

Chapter 29

Alone at my desk I wrote:

Dear Julie, MIss PHd:

You are the most beautiful and captivating woman I have ever known. I'm head over heels infatuated with you. Hit me over the head with your hammer of love.

```
Your Groveling detective,


Morgan Theodore Roosevelt Einstein Hercules
```

I drew a snaking scribble through my letter.

Then I crumpled it and threw it in the waste basket.

Chapter 30

The place looked like a college campus, complete with lawns and young men and women walking with books in their arms, except for the large wall at the entrance that said in huge brass letters:

DELCO Software Company

Land of the Software Giants.

Northern Campus. Please Register at Gate B.

"Which building is it?" I asked Abdul beside me in my old Camaro.

Abdul was studying a small map on waxy paper. "It's next to the Tubbman Memorial to the Good But Dead. Building A." Abdul looked up, found his direction, and pointed to a building about a block away.

Building A was a big black rectangle sitting among trees as if it were the monolith just landed out of the movie 2001.

"Gotcha," I said driving that way.

"These are pretty fancy grounds for a software firm," I said.

Abdul nodded. "Delco is not a software firm. It is a megalithic software empire. It was started in 1987 by Tubbman himself when he launched a little program called Pip-squeak!. It simply sent e-mail down the phone-line from any computer, and made a squeak when you received a message. It was an immediate hit. Everyone bought it. Tubbman made 5 million himself the first year. Ten million the second year. He bought other software and released it over the years, until he now has a strangle hold on the telecommunications software market. Delco netted 5 billion dollars last year. Bill Tubbman is now worth 35 billion dollars."

"Lot of cash," I said.

"It's said he's building a monstrous huge mansion hidden in the mountains complete with caves for art and wines," said Abdul.

"I imagine he also has a few rooms full of mattresses stuffed with money."

"Oh no," corrected Abdul with a matter-of-fact shrug, "All his money is kept in the First Bank of Tubbman."

Chapter 31

We walked up to Building A, next to the Tubbman Memorial to the Good But Dead. It was a small jewel case box set on a black marble pedestal. In the jewel box, encased in clear glass, was a single pin. A sign said that the names of a hundred software engineers who died creating software were engraved on the pin head.

At the entry way, young software servants were pressing credit cards to metal plates and being buzzed in through glass doors. I reached out and tried a door, which didn't budge. Locked. No one looked at us as they walked in and out the glass doors and Abdul and I loitered out on the sidewalk. A small black post stood beside one door and on it hung a telephone receiver.

Abdul walked over and put the receiver to his ear.

"Morgan Hercules and Abdul Dallah. We're here to see Mr. Tubbman. Yes, we are having an appointment. No, I'm not kidding. Yes, we are having one. Well, check it! Yes? Yes? Yes! Morgan Hercules. I'm Abdul Dallah his assistant. I'm making the appointment. No, it is not for charity reasons. Yes. Fine, please be giving me your name, so that when we miss our appointment with Mr. Tubbman, I can be giving him yours. What? Fine, open the door then."

The door buzzed unhappily.

Abdul quickly reached out and pulled it open.

"After you, Boss," he said with a smile.

"Well done," I said.

Chapter 32

A woman in red jacket, the kind a real estate agent might wear, ushered us down several halls and up a flight of stairs carpeted thickly in emerald green. Beaming brass, door knobs, light switches, wall lights, and stair banisters shone brightly everywhere. I was glad Abdul was with me. He'd insisted on coming along because he knew software and so could help with a background understanding of Tubbman and the Delco company. At least it was two of us walking these large hallways.

The woman in red stopped before an elevator doorway. Beside the doorway was a sign that said, "Employees Named Tubbman Only."

She pressed the wall button. Noticing that I had read the sign, the red-jacketed employee smiled and said, "Mr. Tubbman has a sense of humor."

I nodded.

Finally the elevator door opened. With a sweep of her hand, the young woman bid us enter.

We got into the elevator and stood. The door closed.

There was only one button.

I pushed it.

Up we went.

Chapter 33

When Abdul and I stepped out of the confinement of the elevator, we both began glancing around to get oriented. Oddly, just at the entrance way, sitting on a low grey sofa, was a man with heavy jowls and the loose baggy eyes of a bloodhound. He was a heavy man in grey short sleeve shirt. He looked up at us as we stepped out of the elevator almost on his toes. Abdul and I nearly backed up into the elevator again in surprise.

"Yes? I'm Bill Tubbman. CEO of Delco. Can I help you?" said the man. His hands was folded on the book in his lap and he made no effort to stand up or move in anyway as he spoke.

"I'm Morgan Hercules, and this is my assistant Abdul Dallah," I said. Abdul nodded beside me.

Glancing around the rest of the room, I could see many different types of computer terminals, some apparently quite antiquated, set on top of filing cabinets here and there. A single window, near the roof, let in dim light. The blackened room felt like the dark inside of a broom closet with its door left ajar.

Then I noticed against the far wall, just behind Tubbman, was a huge safe with a large dial and spoked hand wheels.

I nodded toward the safe and joked, "Looks like you could keep a cool billion in there."

Tubbman glanced over his shoulder nonchalantly. "No, I don't keep any money in there. We keep GM copies of our software, the Golden Masters, in there. It guards the entire wealth of Delco. And I sit right here before it. The place could burn down, or be hit with a cruise missile, and we wouldn't lose our software. I'm the only one that knows the combination."

"What happens if you forget the combination?" I asked.

"Then I just own a big safe," replied Tubbman without blinking an eye.

"Seems kind of dim in here," I said, looking about.

"Don't mind the surroundings," said Tubbman, "It's an atmosphere in which I do my best work, and so I've grown used to it. I'd never leave it if I didn't have to."

"Thank you for seeing us, Mr. Tubbman," I began.

Tubbman nodded. Something in the slow nod, a granting of permission, told me that Tubbman felt he was someone superior to most. Definitely superior to me.

Before I could go on, Abdul spoke up.

"It is very fine to be meeting you, Mr. Tubbman. You are releasing admirable software. And Delco is doing so amazingly well."

"Yes," said Tubbman.

"We're here to ask you some questions about a man called the Emperor," I said. "He may have given you money of some sort back in 1987."

"No such person exists in the software industry," said Tubbman flatly.

"And I've received no money from him. If that's all you want, I'll be saying good day." Tubbman's shoulders rose as if he might get up ending the conversation.

Abdul jumped in, "But in 1987, isn't it then you were starting up Delco? With the release of your Pip-squeak! program?"

"Yes," said Tubbman, "Up until that time, I'd been looking over software firms to help with their development. I would look at products and then advise firms how they could be improved. I also offered to market other software engineers' work. Then I came up with Pip-squeak! It took off, and here I am," said Tubbman.

I decided to let Abdul take the lead in questioning.

"You see, Boss," said Abdul turning to me, "Mr. Tubbman here is advertising for software products to develop, looking over applications submitted to him for market potential?"

"Yes, I started out that way, until in 1987, I released my own," said Tubbman, looking now squarely at Abdul.

"I'm understanding, however, that your product, Pip-squeak!, is having its roots in another product that was sent for evaluation to you. A small company called Inventions of India, they are sending you a small telecommunications package. Right, Mr. Tubbman?"

"How do you know about Inventions of India?" asked Tubbman, perturbed. "Listen, if you're some kind of lawyer team, you can just meet my own fifty lawyers down the hall."

Abdul looked at me innocently, "You see, it's rumored in the software industry, that Pip-squeak! is actually the product of another small company, which was evaluated by Mr. Tubbman here. Some are even saying stolen and released in revised form."

"How do you know this? This is all foggy legal grounds," said Tubbman. It was obvious Tubbman didn't like the direction the conversation was going.

"Abdul is my computer wiz," I offered inanely.

"Well, he doesn't know what he's talking about," replied Tubbman with a surly inflection.

"In fact, some would say you took this Pip-squeak! software wholesale from the real developer, and even charged a small fee to initially review it," said Abdul mildly.

"At that time, I reviewed many software products, most really bad. Programmed garage door s that could be scheduled. Computer bowling games with digitized bowling alley sounds, including squeaky shoes. A program to keep track of your vaccinations. Worthless junk."

"Excepting, a small telecommunications program submitted to you, right? That eventually became the basis for Pip-squeak!" Abdul was like a bulldog grilling Tubbman. I wondered where all this computer lore came from.

"Have you ever heard of the Emperor?" I broke in.

"No! I said that!" said Tubbman to me heatedly. Then he turned his attentions back to Abdul. "Listen, Pip-squeak! was my product. I don't like the insinuations I hear. I may have seen a lot of products, which lent me a lot of good ideas. But Pip-squeak! was mine."

"You knew once you had a successful product the lawyers could take over to defend it! Defend it against any small under-financed firm called Inventions of Indian! Right? In fact, you took the code and changed the name, I'm guessing."

"Abdul, I don't think we're here for a lesson in computer history," I said, trying to get him off the subject.

Tubbman suddenly stood up. He had a surprisingly squat body.

"Look, you're talking about something you know nothing about!" snarled Tubbman at Abdul.

"I'm knowing the man in India who is claiming to be sending you the program."

"Well, he's never sent a follow-up letter to me!" said Tubbman.

"You're rich. People, they think you are a George Washington or Ghandi or someone. You are not, Mr. Tubbman."

"I don't have time for this," said Tubbman, "Take your little brown man servant here and get off my campus. I've got some important development to do. This interview is finished. And I'm sorry it took place."

"You're nothing but a Mister Moneybags," continued Abdul.

"That's strange coming from a feather-weight rug rider. Who are you to tell me anything?" laughed Tubbman leering face to face with Abdul.

Abdul's eyes were hard and glassy as marbles. Abdul drew a pencil from his front pocket.

"Put this where the sun isn't shining and figure it out," said Abdul.

I winced. My office assistant was telling a billionaire software mogul to shove a pencil up his ass and do some arithmetic.

"Watch out, rug-rider, or I'll buy your home loan and kick you out on your ass."

"My name is Abdul Dallah, the Slave of God. Start fooling with the slave of God, and God gets very pissed," said Abdul staunchly. "And God is owning your home loan, little laddy!"

"Little laddy?" I thought to myself. I knew "little laddy" was the direst insult Abdul ever meant to employ. Reserved for the biggest jerks, it meant this person was beneath contempt.

Tubbman and Abdul continued to stare eyeball to eyeball like two angry pitbulls.

"Uh," I cleared my throat, "That's all for now, Mr. Tubbman. We appreciate your time."

I backed Abdul through the elevator door.

Tubbman didn't say a word, he merely grunted and sat down.

Chapter 34

Back seated with Abdul out in my old Camaro, I looked over and said, "Well, I think that went well. Don't you?"

Chapter 35

"Why did you lay into Tubbman like that?" I said.

"Oh, I've just been hearing that he's making his millions from others, and that this Pip-squeak! program was not really his. He only did a little modifications and camouflaging of the code, then is making millions."

"I gathered that. But we learned nothing about the Emperor. Not even if Tubbman received any money from him. He denied everything."

Abdul remained silent and pensive.

"So why did you do it?"

Abdul shrugged, "Oh, that kind of tubby man is bothering me, I guess."

"Abdul, the rich can be dangerous," I said.

"Oh, Boss, the rich can be shmoos. He is serving nothing but his software and himself. He is not even master of his own greed."

Chapter 36

I knocked on Julie's door. I didn't have a lot to report, but I wanted to see her face to face again. Find out more.

The door opened, and there hung the red dot and crinkling angry eyes of Aunty Dotty, the ever-cordial Indian crone.

As I opened my mouth, the door slammed shut.

Chapter 37

I knocked on Julie's door again. After a long wait, the door opened and there stood Julie.

"Hi," I said.

"Were you waiting here long?" asked Julie, "I just passed Aunty Dotty who said something about putting garbage out in the hall."

"I suppose that would be me," I said.

"Sorry, Morgan, don't let Aunty Dotty bother you," said Julie smiling. "She's just peculiar."

"Peculiar is one word, I can think of others," I said.

Julie led me in to sit on her purple couches in the living room. I caught a glimpse of Anna Elisabeth lumbering into the first door down the hallway and disappearing.

Julie sat back on the couch, taking a knee in her hands, and said, "Well, how'd it go with Bill Tubbman, Billionaire."

"I let Abdul do most of the talking," I said. I didn't say that Abdul had come close to biting the billionaire on the leg.

"We didn't learn a whole lot," I said. "Evidently Abdul believes that a lot of Tubbman's fortunes were built on stolen code. But Tubbman denied hearing of the Emperor. A complete blank."

"So what's next?" asked Julie.

"Next we call on a financial consultant, a John Achmyer. He's here in San Francisco."

"Why him?"

"He was on the FBI list as receiving money from the Emperor. He has a kind of shady past. He may know something. Because you received that note, and some of the people on our list are local, it seems there's some connection with the Emperor here in the City."

"But other than that, you're just feeling in the dark," said Julie.

"Yes."

"Don't you make a theory and then go after proving or disproving it?" asked Julie.

"Nope, we just feel in the dark," I said.

"And that works?" said Julie.

"Everybody starts in the dark," I said with a shrug.

Julie didn't like that answer, but said nothing.

"Julie, do you have any other relationships, outside of your home here?" I asked.

"You mean boyfriends and such? Are you going to ask me out on a date?" Julie had arched an eyebrow and risen back a bit smiling snidely as she said it.

My face went a bit crimson. I wouldn't mind asking her on a date, but I'd actually wanted to know more about her lifestyle. So I was guilty, but not guilty.

"No, I wanted to know more about you, how you live," I said.

"No real relationships. I was pawed a few times in undergraduate school, and didn't appreciate it. I keep rather aloof from my university colleagues, most of whom are married. I verbally slay any football jocks in my classes who cast an eye at me."

"I see," I said. I made a mental note to never wear a sweatshirt in her presence.

"Other than that, I've been very busy these last few years, finishing my work and dissertation. I've been very distant to most."

"No one you know has any reason to play pranks?" I said.

Julie shook her head.

"And Aunty Dotty, you don't seem to know much about her," I said.

Julie stiffened. It was as if I'd accused her of failing a simple exam.

"Well, I can do some research and find dates when she arrived here in the States, if that's what you want. Other than that, my adoption has always been off limits. I've been unable to obtain any information about it. I tried when I was 19, did some calls, but hit a dead end. The adoption agency could not give me any information about my real parents."

"So how did you get that portrait?" I asked.

"Like I said, it just came one day, when I was little."

"You live in a nice apartment here," I said.

"So?" replied Julie.

"Do you pay the rent?"

Julie nodded seeing my drift.

"Aunty Dotty has always paid. She has a pension from the British Government. Her husband died in the military. Second World War."

"And she sent you through college on a military pension?" I asked.

"Well, no," smiled Julie. "I had good grades. And out of the blue, I received full tuition for the school I wanted to attend."

"That's nice, it sounds like you were always a good student," I said.

Julie cast a glance at her Mother's portrait on the wall.

"Yes, I was," she said.

Chapter 38

I sat in silence for a second or two. "Well, I guess I'll get going."

"Okay," said Julie.

"I'll keep you posted as the investigation continues."

"Okay," said Julie.

"I'll see myself out," I said.

"Okay," said Julie.

"Don't let the door hit you in the butt!" came shouted in a crone's voice from down the hall.

"Good hearing," I said.

"Excellent most would say," nodded Julie.

Chapter 39

I took a last glance at the sheet Abdul had printed out on John Achmyer of Achmyer Financial Consultants. Then I put it down on the car seat next to me. I'd parked in front of the place, a big concrete block of a building hunched on a wharf over the San Francisco Bay. Somehow with a financial office over the bay, the place reeked of thievery and smuggling. Or maybe it was just the background sheet of Achmyer's financial dealings that was contaminating my view.

Achmyer had been a lawyer for the mob, but when that wasn't respectable enough, he had opened his own financial consulting agency. His company did large land deals and managed investments. I assumed this meant a good deal of laundering money. Oddly, Achmyer had a fairly good standing in the upper society of the City, even having his photo taken giving checks to the Mayor for local charities.

Almost as a point stressing good standing and important financial commitments, two slim uniformed security guards, complete with shoulder patches, utility belts, and handguns, stood at the glass entry way. One of the security guards opened the door for me as I walked up.

Once inside, I faced a polished semi-circular red marble desktop where a single blond receptionist sat like a sentinel in a foreign outpost.

"May I help you?" asked the young woman. She had a winning smile with lipstick as red as a fire engine.

"Morgan Hercules. I've an appointment with John Achmyer. My assistant made the appointment."

With a nod, the receptionist lifted a phone hand set, pressed a button and listened. She then said, "Morgan Hercules is here." She listened for several seconds as if the secrets of my life were being read back to her. I hoped she wasn't hearing about that Twinky incident back in third grade.

(Twinky + teacher's chair = vast pedigogical error.) She put down the phone and smiled.

"The door to your right," she said pointing.

"Thank you," I said.

I went over to the door and opened it.

"Mr. Hercules, please come in!" shouted a very round-faced man at the far end of the room. He was small and over weight, built something like a bowling ball. This image wasn't helped by the tight black suit he wore, and two black eyes that peered from his nearly bald head.

The office was an immense aviary hung with viney plants and ferns, and here and there carefully positioned sofas with floral patterns. One wall was entirely glass panes looking out across the money-green bay. Silver ashtrays stood here and there. And the floor was covered with a rug colored with huge concentric circles such that I felt I was walking across a target. The round man, who I assumed was Achmyer, motioned me forward waving his hand above his mahogany desk, big enough to be Liberace's piano, complete with silver candelabra on the far corner. Unlit. Next to the desk, sitting in a squat pile, was another security guard, equipped and armed like the ones outside, except this one had the small mean look of a pug Nazi.

"Come in, come in. I understand you're here to find out about someone. A personage called the Emperor?" asked Achmyer.

"Yes," I said. I extended my hand and shook Achmyer's. I let it fall back by itself, because that's what you do with cold undersize fish.

"Please be seated," said Achmyer, motioning to the floral sofa behind me.

I nodded and sat. Achmyer reseated himself at his desk. The security guard to his right only moved uncomfortably, recrossing his legs.

"Actually," I said, "We're not even sure the Emperor exists."

"Oh, he exists," broke in Achmyer, "He may be somewhere in the underworld, but he's there." Achmyer nodded reassuringly.

"Why are you interested in the Emperor?" asked Achmyer.

"Well, I've a client. I'm a private investigator, as my assistant probably informed you. My client is very interested in contacting the Emperor."

"So would many, I believe," smiled the round-face man. I noticed that although he was nearly bald, there was three pencil-lines of hair going across his head. Atleast they may have been hair, or just pencil lines, I couldn't tell.

"We have reason to believe you may know something of the Emperor," I said.

"Why is that?" Achmyer asked.

"We received a list of contacts who had received funds from the Emperor, back in 1987. You were on the list."

"Amounts, dates?" asked Achmyer, bending forward with curiosity.

"No, merely your name as a recipient."

Achmyer leaned back relaxing, "And you're not with the government?"

"I suppose if I was, I'd say no, and if I wasn't, I'd say no," I said.

"So you didn't say," said Achmyer. "Well, it matters little, we're in the clear here. All our dealings are strictly above board. But the Emperor does interest us. I did have contact with him once, as you say, way back in the late 80's. I'd be very interested in picking up our discussions where they left off...And might even make it worth your while should you help find him."

"I was hoping you'd help me," I said. "Just exactly what was your dealing with the Emperor?"

Achmyer sat back jovially and threw up his hands.

"He was interested in a large purchase. The Cayman islands."

"You mean he wanted to buy an entire island?" I asked.

Achmyer smiled as if at a penniless non-comprehending boob. I returned an encouraging boob-like nod.

"No, he wanted to purchase the Caymen islands. The country."

"You've got to be kidding," I said.

Achmyer gave me an evil smile and sat up with a happy wave of his hand. "Oh, no. No one was kidding. The money to do it showed up. I did some checking, transferred some funds from a Swiss Bank account number I'd been given to make the purchase. I saw the numbers were real. It was a real proposition."

"So, I went right to work on it. I put out word to the right people. I set up negotiations with the head man in the Caymans in quiet. I thought at the time I was dealing with Arab Sheiks. But the money was there. I wasn't asking more questions."

"How do you arrange to buy a country?" I asked.

Achmyer interlaced his fingers and posed them over his chest in a gesture of false-modesty before speaking.

"It does take a few phone calls. To people in the right places. I have connections that know how to do these things. It wasn't long before I had a deal in sight. We'd pay off a list of the government heads, then purchase as much property as legally possible, then, of course, there were those who would resist. Several in the military, a list of maybe 50 civilians. I realized we'd have to stage a coup, so I put together some overthrow plans for a small mercenary force to launch from Central America. I'd called in some favors at the NSA, in D.C., and soon had the names of qualified individuals. I also have some influence with other organizations, the type that like to set up gambling casinos and such. It would only take four months to put together the landing party, fully equipped, Russian-made guns and armor. I figured we'd snatch the country total for about $25 billion. I had half that in the Swiss bank account already."

Achmyer cleared his throat, getting excited about the prospects. "I think I had the Caymen islands in the Emperor's pocket, with a pretty healthy commission in mine. What's a billion here or there, among owners of small countries?"

"What happened?" I said.

Achmyer frowned. "I don't know. I sent the final plan, and the hit list off for approval. The next day, the money dried up. Nothing in the account. And a note comes to me via telegram from Geneva: Stop Caymen Islands Investment. Or add your name to list. The Emperor."

"And that was that?" I said.

"The money was gone. No take over possible," shrugged Achmyer. "But, let me tell you. I learned the Caymen islands would come cheap. If I could ever field another investor."

Achmyer shook his bald head regretfully, a little like someone spinning a bowling ball to find the holes.

"This Emperor sure had some dough. I'd never had any direct contact with him. All communications came from phone voices, telegrams, and such. So I couldn't recontact him to put the plan in the correct light. Just the financial follow-up was real. Big bucks."

"Any guesses how he came about it?" I said.

Achmyer shook his head, "Only rumor mill grindings, something about his making real money, dollar, marks, and francs whenever he wants."

"False paper?" I asked.

"Just a rumor of counterfeiting. But no government has declared any..."

I rose to leave. "Thank you, Mr. Achmyer."

"Say," said Achmyer with a false smile. "I've been forthcoming with you. Should you actually contact the Emperor? Remind him of me? Here's my card. Give me a call. That Caymen island deal is still there. This Emperor, he had the bucks. A big chunk could come your way."

"You seem to like the idea of all that money," I said.

"Well, you could hit me over the head with a gold brick and I'd like it," laughed Achmyer.

Achmyer had been shaking my hand as he said this. It was all I could do not to pull it away, as if an office shredder machine had caught my coat sleeve and was making ready to pull me in.

Chapter 40

I got into my old Camaro and putted away from the curb.

Well, unlike the Emperor, as head of Morgan's Eagle-Eye Detective Agency, I won't be purchasing one of the Caymen islands soon.

Chapter 41

Not a lot of my work results in any real money.

But then I got off the money scale years ago. I stopped measuring myself in terms of cash, don't build my day around how much I'm making an hour. I measure my success in terms of the spirit. My feelings of the spiritual, of being on the spiritual path, are the only things of real value anyway. I value doing things that allow me to kick back and have a Snickers bar and a beer at the end of the day and feel good about it.

My real work is what I do for free.

Chapter 42

Emperor's Comment:

Morgan just means that on the grand scale he's paying for his life with the cosmic currency.

Chapter 43

I wondered: was the Emperor making money, that is, as a counterfeiter par excellence? A rogue outside of society who just found it easier to print money than earn it?

Chapter 44

Emperor's Comment:

Bah, Morgan! Outside of society? My counterfeiting operation is a natural extension of capitalism. In capitalism, the person creates an object and tries to sell it for more than it's worth. The more your get for a product the better, until people won't buy it. The point is the pointless amassing of cash. Big corporations with big bank accounts. I do the same, just on an extreme level. I take many little bits of paper of very low value and print on them in such a way that they are each worth a $1,000 dollars. I'm simply overcharging like everyone else.

Chapter 45

"Hello, Julie?" I said to the phone.

"Yes, hello, who is this?" answered Julie.

"It's me, Morgan. I wanted to give you a little status report."

"Any progress?"

"Very little, I'm afraid. I met with a financier on the bad side of town. John Achmyer. He's on the list of people the Emperor has contacted. He did seem to have had some dealings with the Emperor, but mainly through fronts and indirect communications. No direct leads. In fact, Achmyer gave me his card in case we contact the Emperor," I hesitated, "In order to pursue a business deal." I didn't mention the business deal meant the resting away of an entire archipelago in the Caribbean, complete with hit list.

"Any feeling for who this Emperor is, as bad as they say?"

"Let's just say he's a big spender," I said. "And he may really know how to make money. I don't know how reliable the information from this Achmyer is."

"What's next?" asked Julie. "You do have a plan or something."

"We call on the next name on our list," I said.

Chapter 46

I met Abdul at Gate 69 at San Francisco International Airport. We were scheduled to get on United, flight #89, to Honolulu. I had a small sports bag of underwear and toiletries with me. No gun. I'd had to leave that at home, mainly because of the airport metal detectors, not really because of the security guards who were often so bored they were nearly sightless.

Abdul waved as he saw me approach the gate.

"Here are the tickets, Boss. I have the boarding passes already."

I nodded thanks.

"Do you think we'll really get to see her?" I said, still doubtful.

The evening before, Abdul had spotted a blurb in the SF Chronicle that Mother Teresa would be visiting Hawaii, and was invited to tour the secret island of Nihau. This was the small island reserved only for full-blooded Hawaiian's. It was just off the Northwest side of Kauai. No one went there, white-faces, anyway, without an expressed invitation. Mother Teresa was evidently being honored to come see the sacred grounds.

"Oh, we can only be hoping," said Abdul. "But I'm thinking maybe yes. I know when she gets into the airport. There's a chance."

I nodded.

"How did we pay for the plane tickets?" I asked. I knew Julie's small finances couldn't afford to send two investigators off on a quick trip to Hawaii.

"I did some trading of Frequent Flier miles on the computer," said Abdul. "The whole thing is costing us one dollar and twenty-two cents. I can pay that if you want. For my neighbor, Julie."

I shook my head no.

I bought a paper at the newsstand and then Abdul and I boarded the plane for a five-hour flight.

Our hope was to somehow intercept Mother Teresa at the Honolulu International and ask her a few questions. We didn't expect it to be easy to get the woman to grant us time, seeing that she probably would be behind a damn of guards and well-wishers. But I had admitted it was worth a try.

Abdul knew the gate where she would be getting off the plane. We'd be there an hour ahead of her.

The takeoff was excellent, and we settled back for a long trip in an airbus.

About mid-flight, I began grazing through the paper as Abdul contentedly listened to his head phones with eyes closed.

Something caught my eye on the inside page, and I elbowed Abdul awake.

"Look at this," I whispered.

Abdul leaned over the armrest to see the article I was pointing at. It was three columns and a photograph of a extremely outraged man being stuffed into a police car.

The article read:

Tubbman Software Empire Collapses, Tubbman Has Fit.

by Bill Morris

Financial thunder struck today as the Delco Software Corp was successfully captured in a hostile takeover. Long known as the most-moneyed software giant in the computer industry, Delco was overrun by the EMPER Finances' surprise bid of $50 per share which secured 51% of outstanding Delco shares. The previous day Delco shares had been selling at $25.23.

A representative of the EMPER group stated that Delco would be broken up and sold for full worth over the next two months. Bids were welcome. The first

order of business would be the firing of
Bill Tubbman as board director, and CEO
of Delco.

"Preposterous!" was Tubbman's cry as he
admitted loss of control of the company.
Tubbman, visibly upset, had been unable
to shield his company from the takeover,
which had occurred in several hours.

"Someone just flushed us out with
money!" cried Tubbman to reporters. The
total amount of purchase was estimated at
12 billion dollars. At that time Tubbman
was taken ill, vomiting repeatedly on
nearby reporters. Attendants hastily
rushed him into a police vehicle for
transport to the Goldenvale hospital.

I looked over at Abdul as he read smiling to himself.

"Now I am one happy rug rider," Abdul said.

Chapter 47

You might ask why I want to be a detective. I believe it is because I was once lost as a kid.

When I was four or five, my mother had taken me to a zoo. I remember being in knee-pants and suspenders, with a little black cap on my young head. My mother was in a long gray overcoat, even though the Spring weather was balmy. I was entranced with the animals. Instead of old lions limping arthritically in their cages, bald spots showing through their fur like worn out rugs, I saw magnificent animals, kings of ferocity! I was a well-groomed kid that minded his manners, and so was really into ferocious beasts. You know how kids get into dinosaurs that actually represent all that repressed youth, that energy that actually wants to knock the house down. When I saw a rhino, I saw a Sherman tank, and if I could just hop on, I could drive that baby through a wall! Other kids would yell "Yah, Rinny!" to their Rin-Tin-Tin-like German shepherds. I wanted to yell, "Yah, Rhino!" as I rode, Tarzan jogging by on his jungle Cadilac!

My mother took me by the hand and led me from cage to cage. I remember her buying me a small bag of popcorn, and I was small enough to want to feed the pigeons by throwing a handful down on their heads in a shotgun blast.

I saw gibbons and howlers looping about inside their cages like remote control boomerangs flying around.

Spring in the zoo! A marvelous walking adventure.

My mother gave her careful smile, always cautioning me not to get too close to the animals. Little did I know. Now, after forty, I am still figuring out what it means to be too close to the animals.

I wanted to go and see a crazy chimpanzee that I'd seen once in the primate house. His name was Max Bananaman III. He was one grody chimp, throwing feces at passersby and chattering with laughter as we unsuspecting zoo visitors dodged and jumped. Surprise!

My mother cautioned me to wait here one minute. She looked down at the paved ground indicating the sacred circle of her intention. I knew telepathically, as a five year old, if I moved from this spot, I would be thrust into another life, another dimension that I knew nothing about.

"Freeze in place," was my mother's stern eye-ball command. I did.

She left for a nearby fountain to go wash something from her hands. I saw her purse flopping on her side as she walked hurriedly away. She was pressing her steps to get back to me quickly.

There was a line at the drinking fountain.

I saw a peacock feather in a hole under a hedge. It had a wonderful purple eye. I left the magic circle. I rushed to go get it.

When my mother came back, I was gone.

When I came out of the hedge, dragging my colorful feather, she was gone.

I was alone in a big zoo, surrounded by caged animals, and aimless wandering humans like myself. I realized there wasn't much point in this without my mother!

I took my feather and went to see Mad Max. Max was his normal shit throwing self. I wondered if I could be like him. I wondered if he could be like me. Would he wear knee-pants, suspenders, and a little cap? Would he look like a hairy me?

Then I thought I'd better go find my mother. I was nothing without her. Really. I was dreams and ambitions and an uneducated little boy. All real substance came from my mother.

I started wandering around the zoo, looking left and right, careful to hold my feather with its deep purple eye high over my head. I suppose I thought this had some magic power to call in my mother.

I walked here. I walked there. I looked at the animals, all living their lives indifferent to me. I suddenly had the striking insight for a five-year-old that they were all mother-less animals just like me. And here they were walking around in cages.

I think I may have made one circuit of the zoo. A lot of walking for small legs. My mother, who was frantically looking high and low for me, had somehow missed me.

I sat down beside a garbage can on the edge of the zoo. Then I saw a little patch of inviting grass nearby between two bushes. I went and lay down there and went to sleep.

When I woke up, it was dark.

I looked around. Darkness everywhere! And there, wobbling about the darkness were big shiny white eyes, tracking light back and forth around the zoo. I heard shouts! Men's deep guttural voices shouting my name.

Zookeepers come to get me into a cage!

I was scared. I gripped my feather so hard I kinked it. The bravest thing I could think of to do was cry. A couple of tear dripped from my cheek.

Men in the zoo were after me and calling my name! Good God, did they have the cage ready? Would I have to take my knee-pants off and run bare-naked in a cage? Morgan, wolf-child of the big city jungles!

I saw three hulking figures about fifty feet away, stooping and poking under the bushes with broom handles. They were working their way toward me.

Quietly, I got up. I was going to get away. I didn't want to be a zoo animal. I crouched and duck-walked, occasionally putting my hand down on sticky ground, as I waddled away under the hedge. To my right was a big black structure. It was the size of a barn and looked like refuge. I instinctively went in that direction, homing in on shelter. When I came out of the hedge at the side of the building, I found a big black door. Amazingly, when I tried it, it pulled open.

I stepped into an ominous black cavern. I stood shivering and breathing quickly for a minute, still holding my purple peacock feather gripped tight in my hand.

As I stood, my eyes adjusted to the dim light coming in through high windows around the room. The place smelled, a fleshy dank smell of old food and damp hair. I saw long stretches of bars that ran to the ceiling. It was like a great hallway fenced with bars. I could see my way to walk a bit. I stepped over to one side and looked in a cage. I could only see a big black lump in a corner.

This really troubled me. I could feel my face rumpling up with tears. I was alone and no one was with me. My mother gone. Gruff men after me. Stuck in this place. I whimpered a bit. I put my hand out on the cage bar to steady myself. Then under tons of self-pity, I collapsed to the floor. I sat with my feather in my lap and cried.

Exhausted I fell asleep again.

The next morning, light was filling the high ceiling windows. I woke blinking, feeling a warm hand on me. As I roused myself, still not aware of where I was, I felt a deep comfort from this weight on my shoulder. It was a weight like the hand of my mother. When I finally looked over, I saw a thick black hand with dirty fingernails. I looked up, and there beside my face were the intent eyes of an old mountain gorilla. I looked. And the gorilla looked back at me. And I remember such an intense look of concern in this animal's black eyes.

Its hand rose and fell on my shoulder several times.

I was strangely reassured about life.

I got up and gave this old mother my pet feather. As the gorilla took my feather and began inspecting it, I looked long at her in her cage, and then I walked outside.

I was rushed at by a circle of Zookeepers who captured me and took me to my real mother.

I think that's why I want to be a detective.

After being so terribly lost, now all I want to do is find things.

Chapter 48

Emperor's Comment:

Ha. So Morgan, the great master detective is really the servant of the small and lost. Ha. Ha. Ha.

Chapter 49

I remember now, during one of our conversations on a long afternoon with nothing to do, Abdul once telling me something wise his father had said. His father was explaining the differences between the English and Indian cast systems and the meaning of being an untouchable.

Mr. Dallah said, "We are all slaves. But, you can choose your master."

Chapter 50

We arrived in Honolulu, the air, even in the airport, sweet with topical flowers. Parades of people in flowery shirts and leis walked to and fro, lazily porting suitcases. I heaved a happy sigh to be off the plane. Abdul had rushed off to reserve accommodations at a local condominium on the beach. He said a travel agent had given him a ticket for a $10.00 one night stay in off-season. It was a new place and the office was anxious to sell condos, thus the cheap rates for prospective buyers. I took this in as a natural extension of Abdul's money genius; we had decided to sleep over before taking the next five-hour flight home in the morning.

Abdul and I next headed over to reconnoiter the gate where Mother Teresa would deplane.

Although we had an hour, the place was packed. A jungle of flash cameras was held by news people like periscopes at ready. Crowds of crisply dressed clergy were clustered in groups, and nuns and even monks were chattering together. And the kids! We had a little playground of over-dressed floral five-to-ten-year-olds sitting on seat backs and jumping from window sills.

"This ain't going to be easy," I said.

Abdul nodded looking sternly over the crowded.

"They say she has a weakness for the children," said Abdul.

I looked left and saw a small alcove leading to an airport men's room. Judging the path of passengers from the docked plane, Mother Teresa and her entourage would have to walk directly past it.

I motioned Abdul to follow and we stepped into the little bathroom entryway. I looked at him and said, "Prepare yourself, I doubt we'll get much chance to catch her attention."

Abdul nodded. His chin stiffened, which I know is a good sign.

It's a little like the hair going up on the back of a pit bull.

About twenty minutes later quite a hubbub stirred the crowd as Mother Teresa's airplane was spotted floating down from the clouds.

I looked at Abdul and we both tensed.

Fifteen minutes later, as the gate door swung open, we heard the first reporters shouting down the hall. I looked out to see a crowd jamming the door way, and a small old woman, with what looked like a wide white handkerchief draped over her head, walking toward them. It was the slow-paced walk of the old, but not one of the infirm. I saw fathers in flower shirts lifting children up over their heads.

"Mother Teresa, Mother Teresa!" The calls raised like flags over the crowd.

Priests were wiggling toward the front of the group like pollywogs.

I took a deep breath. I hadn't a clue what I would say.

The crowd, completely concealing the small old woman in white, was now moving towards us.

Flash bulbs were going off over Mother Teresa's head in a miniature lightening storm. I caught glimpses of her face, which was looking down, nodding, and not too happy. Everyone was vying for her.

With dismay, I realized I would be next.

The crowd was before us now and I could see the old woman, spindly, but unbend, walking by a few feet away.

"Mother Teresa!" I shouted, "I must talk with you!" I saw no visible response.

It was then Abdul called out something in Hindi, his native tongue.

Mother Teresa stopped, turned her head our way, hesitating.

"Mother Teresa," I shouted, "I must talk with you! It concerns the death of a child!"

The crowd stopped as Mother Teresa looked my way, finding Abdul and I among the crowd.

Then I realized she was pushing towards us.

"The death of a child?" said the old woman approaching us. I was a bit befuddled for an answer. But Abdul stepped forward, put his arm around the old woman's shoulder and we walked her into the men's room.

Instantly, I felt bodyguards rushing behind us in a wave.

Inside the ceramic lair of the men's room, Abdul and I were pushed up against walls and frisked as Mother Teresa protested.

Finally we were deposited before the Saint like a couple of kids for discipline.

I looked over at Abdul who was bowing deeply at the waist.

"Why not?" I thought and bowed as well.

Chapter 51

"What's this business about a dying child?" asked Mother Teresa. "Stop bowing you fools, I'm not God." She looked on us with her old woman's bony face and beaked nose, serious but without disdain. I took a breath, I knew this stuff about a dying "child" was a stretch; but it was all I could think of to get her attention.

"My name is Morgan, Morgan Hercules, Mother. I'm an investigator, and this is my partner, Abdul Dallah."

Mother Teresa looked over closely at Abdul now risen from his fast-bowing mode. Something in the old woman's eyes brightened keenly as she looked at him.

"We are trying to locate a man. A woman-child is sick. She'll die unless we find a bone marrow donor. We hoped you might help us," I said a bit breathlessly.

"How can I help?" asked the woman calmly.

"We are looking for the father. But we don't know who he is, exactly. We know you may have had some contact or dealing with him, perhaps in your fundraising."

Abdul gave me a warning glance.

The old woman with the blue-lined handkerchief straightened.

"Mr. Hercules, we don't do fundraising. My order, The Missionaries of Charity, we don't raise funds. We offer the opportunity to share God's love."

"I'm sorry," I said, sensing some offense. "The man we are looking for is sometimes called the Emperor..."

"Never heard of him," was the reply.

I could see by Abdul's face that he was worried I was leading the interview the wrong way.

"Mother, Holy Mother, if you could help us, we are desperate to save this girl. She is a simple Down syndrome child. She can't be saving herself."

Mother Teresa looked over then smiled upon Abdul. "You know, young man, Abdul, you remind me of someone. Your face, it has the same lines as the Madonna of Lentice, from my old Albanian homeland...I loved that statue. It was an inspiration to me in my youth. A darkened woman's face with a child at her shoulder."

Mother Teresa turned to me, "Morgan, instead of fund-raising many people approach us. Once a man approached me with the same question, he had property to offer my order, and he wondered how we handled our finances and our budget." Mother Teresa sighed, "I asked him why he was giving us this property. He replied because it was an urge from within. I told him, well there were many people like him who came to me with the same feeling. To give from within. I told him that was my budget."

I nodded. Here was an old lady who didn't care a fig about money.

Mother Teresa looked over again at Abdul.

"Now what do you want to ask me?" she smiled.

"We think the man we are looking for may have sent you money. Did you receive any notable donations around 1987?"

"We received many, young man. After that Nobel Peace Prize foolishness, my order received many checks. I even remember once in the summer of 1987 in Calcutta, a heavy box was delivered to our Mother House. It was addressed to me! I opened it, and there, stacks of American dollars. My helpers counted it, it was a disconcerting amount to have in our hands!"

"How much was it?" I asked.

"250 million dollars, all in thousand dollar bills," said the old woman without a qualm.

I looked at Abdul, "Did you have any idea who sent it?"

Mother Teresa shook her head, "No, I had no idea. All I knew was there were going to be a lot of little children who ate French fries and wore Adidas for the first time."

Mother Teresa laughed. A Saint with a sense of humor.

"You see, I work for God. People accuse me of being a saint. It's ridiculous! I'm just a woman who works with the poorest of the poor. I'm more God's slave than saint or master. Really. God's love must be shared with all. I start with the poor and dying. It is a large family to take care of."

I nodded.

Mother Teresa was about to end our interview, when she turned on Abdul.

"Don't I know you?" asked Mother Teresa.

"No!" said Abdul, shaking his head hard.

"Yes, I've seen you before. Long ago. It was when I had returned to my old haunts in Darjeeling, India. Someone, a girl was dying."

"No, Mother," Abdul said, "You are mistaken."

"You were much younger, just a boy, 18 or 19. I remember! I was visiting a house where an English girl was dying. She had been abandoned by her family there in Darjeeling. I was revisiting the Sisters of Loreto, where I had been an initiate so many years ago. You were there. Roxanna! Her name was Roxanna, and she died of cholera."

Abdul's brows were knit and his face was intensely red.

"No, Mother," he insisted.

"It isn't nice to lie to Mother Teresa," chided the old woman, not to be budged from her train of thought. "I remember I was in a hut with Roxanna helping when she died, and you were standing in the doorway, holding your poor baby and crying your heart out. I had not been so moved since I had heard God's call to my work."

"No, Mother it was not me," stated Abdul. He was staring intensely at the linoleum flooring. His face was stormy red.

Mother Teresa sighed and turned. The body guards swept her out of sight.

Chapter 52

As we drove to our Hawaiian condo resort, Abdul was unnaturally quiet. Our taxi drove into a super-plush, fern-laden, swaying palm-tree grove-surrounded condominium complex. A rich architect's version of tropical paradise.

After signing in and receiving a key, with only one or two questioning glances at two grown men checking in with handbags for luggage (I was asked where we came from, and my reply "San Francisco" seemed to resolve all further queries), we walked into an amazingly furnished suite. The accommodations were enough to perk anyone's spirits. Especially remembering that Abdul had obtained them for $10.00 a night. It was the kind of suite where you open the refrigerator and find it packed with drinks, cheeses, and even a wide variety of fruits. No Travel Lodge hot chocolate for us! An overhead fan was turning lazily over an expensive brace of furniture, lamps, and inch-deep rug. The condo had a back verandah that opened directly on a beach so white and fine, it was almost a rug of salt. I suspected it might even have been bleached. I was eager to get out and take a walk, get some thinking done.

Abdul and I unpacked in our separate bedrooms. Abdul had still spoken nary a word.

Before I went out, I asked Abdul why he was so quiet.

He shrugged and told me because we had basically found out nothing from Mother Teresa.

I nodded, "Don't worry, we'll keep working on it."

Chapter 53

In shirtsleeves, I went out for a beach-walk among red lava statues that posed like models. I saw sea turtles bobbing in green brine. Tropical birds in rainbow colors hopped under sway-back palms. Surfers plunged and fell out in the ocean waves. And wonderful brown tourist women were lounging on the beach in shoestring bikinis.

The air was balmy, pleasurably moist and warm, with green volcanic hills and mountains always haunting the background.

"Mother Teresa, what a tireless worker for us humans," I thought. Abdul had done a computer search filling me in slightly on the woman's background. A rich merchant, her father Kole had been an Albanian patriot and stern disciplinarian. Her mother, Drana, an indomitable, hardworking woman dedicated to God and caring for the sick and poor and Christian goodworks. Her father died when Agnes (aka Mother Teresa) was eight. Strong, but absent Father (dead), plus strong religiously-dedicated mother, equals Agnes Bojaxhiu: nun. Equals Mother Teresa.

She became a dedicated servant to the lowly, the poor, the sick, the abandoned, the despairing, the dying. For that she received the Nobel Peace Prize and the annointment of sainthood by the ones she served.

We saw her as a master when she saw herself as a servant.

Yet, like so many, was she one more person unconsciously rebuilding her family and its values, just on a supreme scale? If she walked under my detective office window, would my flower pot teeter and fall?

And I wondered as I looked around me, seeing paradise, the greenery and craggy lava rocks, the sea birds, the flowing white sand, the svelte beach skins of women bathers, all a tropical recipe for paradise for the mind and human desire: Mother Teresa, could she see this, too? Did she care so much for our species that she couldn't see the larger wonderful works?

Could she see these little birds with the rainbow-color tails?

Chapter 54

When I re-entered our condo by the verandah glass door, Abdul was sitting with his back to me at the small dining table. With the curtains drawn, the room was darkened. Abdul was bent over the table, his head and shoulders bobbing as if eating a fast bowl of rice.

"Abdul?" I said, stepping onto the cushy rug with pleasure.

Abdul neither turned my way nor replied.

Curious, I stepped around the table to look at him.

Then I saw why his head and shoulders were bobbing. His face to the table surface, he was silently sobbing with all his might.

"Abdul?" I said.

Abdul was having trouble pulling in a breath to acknowledge me.

"Mother Teresa," I said, "She did know you. She'd seen you before. In India."

Rising to an elbow, Abdul wiped at his face with his bare hand.

"Yes, Boss."

"But I thought you grew up in Edinburgh?" I asked.

"Oh, it's a long story. I did grow up there, with my mother. But then at 18 I was sick of it. Sick of being the untouchable boy in the British caste system. The Scottish boys, you know, they can be quite cruel to foreigners. Even if you were nearly born there. By 18, I was just sick of it. So I got some money and left. I went alone to my homeland, to my family's home village, near Darjeeling in Bengal."

"When I got to Darjeeling, I had practically nothing. But Darjeeling was a beautiful place, in the shadow of the Himalayas, surrounded by the ranges of Bhutan and Sikkim, the hills of Nepal. I was poor. But I was a happy lad to be there. Boss, I had ten rupees, but I was so very very glad to be in my own homeland, I gave away five to the poor."

"That makes you a Mother Teresa," I said.

"Oh no," replied Abdul taking me seriously, "When Mother Teresa started her order, she had only five rupees and she gave away *four* to the poor."

He looked at me squarely to tell me the difference was clearly exponential.

"So I built a grass hut, on land that was not mine. It had a dirt floor. I found a job repairing bicycles. I did so for two rupees a week. I could only afford rice and salt!"

"But then, I met Roxanna," Abdul's voice lifted a note.

"Darjeeling was the summer headquarters of the Bengal government. The pish and tosh of the British elite came there to summer. There were grand parties, and the poorest Indian peasants could find jobs."

"One day, in the bicycle shop, I met a girl. A beautiful British girl. So blond. So smiling. And so very kind."

I could see Abdul was there, in Darjeeling, in his mind.

"She simply said hello to me. She spoke to me first. We became friends. We met in parks. And we became very good friends, you know? She was so kind. I was soon heads and tails over her."

"And most amazing, she is also liking me," Abdul's chin rose with this spoken wonder.

"You became close?" I asked.

"Love Mightily, so sayeth the Lord," smiled Abdul. Then he added, "I don't know which Lord said that, but it was one of the good ones..."

"In fact, it came that I must be marrying her. It was necessary, you know? And so I did."

Abdul shook his head.

"But her family, they completely rejected this. They could not have me marrying Roxanna. When they found we had married, it was too late, they completely abandoned her. You know, the British can be very cruel. Even to their own daughters."

"So Roxanna, she came to be living with me. Imagine, in a grass hut! And without a rupee to spend. Yet, we were happy. Roxanna, she seemed exhilarated, free from her family. She made plans to become a teacher, and I to repair more bicycles, someday maybe have my own shop."

"We lived this way two years. I mean we were dirt poor. I mean real dirt, Boss."

"Then she catches cholera. I didn't know what to do. It got worse and worse, until..." Abdul buttoned his lip and shook his head.

"Mother Teresa?" I asked.

"Yes, at the end, Mother Teresa was coming. She came in our hut and took care of Roxanna. She washed Roxanna, and brought her clean water to drink. It was at the very last. Then Roxanna died."

Abdul looked silently at the table for several seconds, then looked up.

"And Boss, I swore that moment I would never be a poor man again. You see, cholera, that is a poor man's disease. It comes from dirt and bad water. I swore I would do everything to never be poor again."

I raised an eyebrow.

"But..." sighed Abdul.

Swallowing dryly, Abdul looked over at me.

"That old saint, she remembered. She remembered me. And she remembered Roxanna. After 42 years."

Abdul's chin quivered. Then his shoulders shook. And as he lay his face back down on the cool table surface and wept, I put my hand on his quaking shoulder.

I said, "Cry it out, Bother. It's the only way."

Chapter 55

Emperor's Comment:

Abdul, he was such a poor blighter. I'm so rich, I don't even remember what it means to be rich.

Chapter 56

On the flight home, Abdul sat with his eyes closed, listening as if in deep mediation to unheard music clamped by headphones to his ears.

I wondered about my recent discoveries about Abdul. I realized I knew so little about him, and we'd shared the same office, master and office-slave for years. Unlooked for discoveries often tilted my world.

Chapter 57

I'd just finished all this pondering when our Boeing 747 touched down in San Francisco. It was good to be home, even if it was kind of a circus.

Chapter 58

I called Julie and set up a lunch meeting. She agreed to meet me at Max's Opera on Van Ness. I was standing by the glass deli cases that showed off the daily cuisine, cakes, and garnishings, as Julie came in. She was dressed in banana-yellow skirt and blouse. Heads actually turned around the restaurant as she entered. She made no sign of noticing as she gave me a small wave and smile.

I love women who do that when they see you.

After a five-minute wait, Julie and I were seated. We both ordered the meatloaf sandwich.

"So you're already back from Hawaii, were you successful? Did you see Mother Teresa?" asked Julie.

"Yes, rather unbelievably, we did. Abdul was a key mover there. He called out in Hindi to her, and we got her attention. Then her body guards kind of slammed us into a bathroom and we had a meeting."

"What did you find out?"

"Well, some surprising things," I said. "She had received a huge donation from someone I think was the Emperor."

"For a criminal master-mind, that seems out of character, religious donations," said Julie.

"True. But people often have more than one side. We're rarely just criminals, artists, or Ph d.'s."

"Or detectives," inserted Julie just to keep us even.

"Right. But this Emperor, if it was him, is enormously wealthy. And that means tremendous power, if you don't hesitate to work outside the law."

"Did Mother Teresa give any details about him?"

"No, she couldn't. We've come up blank for direct contacts."

"Nothing else?" asked Julie.

"Well, yes. Something surprising. I don't know if you knew this, but Abdul had met Mother Teresa before. In India. He'd married, and his wife died. Evidently they were extremely poor. Mother Teresa attended his wife's dying."

"Abdul?" asked Julie incredulously.

I nodded.

"I knew he'd grown up in Edinburgh," I continued, "But I didn't know this part of his married life. He was quite affected by seeing Mother Teresa again."

"I always just thought of him as an old bachelor," said Julie.

"Me, too," I said.

"What happened?" asked Julie. "in India, I mean?"

"Well, I think you should ask him. It's a love story. I'm not too good with those."

"I bet," said Julie. "Morgan, can I ask you something?"

"Sure," I said bunching my shoulders to signify a yes.

"Do you think of me just as a Ph.D.?" asked Julie.

If I told her I thought she was more thrilling than the Queen of Bikinis I knew I was in big trouble. Real big.

"I don't think anyone in this room does," I said.

Julie looked at me squarely, "Well, watch what you think."

I looked at her, saw her face go a bit stern. Message sent. I didn't reply.

"Next, we call on another individual on our list," I said, getting back to business.

"And who is this person? Savory or otherwise?"

"Otherwise. He's a leader in the Ku Klux Klan."

"Just wonderful," said Julie.

Chapter 59

I sat down in my office to read over Abdul's background information about Joseph Hateplum before my trip. The radio was turned on in the corner to mood music, mainly for growing flowers. As I sat, a news break came on that caught my attention:

"Today, in Honolulu Hawaii, an attempt was made to kidnap the renowned missionary worker, Mother Teresa. Man!" drawled the newscaster, voicing his incredulity at the attempt. "Mother Teresa was shaking hands, surrounded by a crowd of well-wishers at the Honolulu airport."

"According to witnesses, a black limousine pulled to the curb and a well-dressed man in a suit approached Mother Teresa, offering a paper that appeared to be a check. Then a disturbance broke out behind Mother Teresa and her guards moved quickly to quell the ruckus. At that instant, the suited man grabbed Mother Teresa's arm and attempted to pull her into the limousine."

My forehead had wrinkled with concern.

The announcer's voice lifted with pleasure, "But this would-be kidnapper didn't know what he was in for with this feisty nun who'd lived decades in the slums of Calcutta. Evidently Mother Teresa began to struggle, throwing a mean right cross at her pursuer's eye, the whole time shouting, "For God's Love! For God's Love!" Evidently, she bopped her surprised assailant pretty good and he let go and grabbed his face."

Now even I was smiling.

"The crowd, angered, moved forward to help Mother Teresa. The assailant had nearly all his clothes ripped from his body before he gained refuge in the limousine and sped off."

The news announcer broke into a chatty tone, "Now why on earth would anyone try to kidnapped a missionary Saint? Especially one with a good right cross." The announcer laughed. You could almost hear him shaking his head in amazement.

Someone had underestimated an old crusader's strength and tenacity.

I shook my head myself. In my mind, I could hear her war cry.

"For God's Love! For God's Love!"

Chapter 60

I arrived in Poughdunk Alabama. It'd taken me some time to drive my bright red rental down the twisty dirt roads to reach the little backwater. It was still early morn, the dew a thick glassy blanket on the grass. I hoped to catch Joseph Hateplum at home before he went to work.

I'd reviewed Abdul's backgrounder on the Grand High Wizard of the Poughdunk Ku Klux Klan. He'd been the fourth son of a junkyard manager who didn't cotton to "pencil learnin" for his sons or himself. He'd had a hundred acres of cars collapsed like accordions from collisions. His children had grown up mean and free to climb over the wreckage of many bad decisions. He referred to anything he didn't like as "a damned import." This included kikes, wops, niggers, and his own kids.

Joseph's three older brothers were bullies, and until he was seven years old, they'd called him "Nigger Joe" and whenever they felt like it, as a kind of family joke, had bopped him on the top of the head with their fists like driving a circus tent stake.

Then the whole family would stand around and laugh.

I'm sure this did wonders for little Joseph's self-esteem.

[FBI files on Grand High Wizards are tremendously detailed.]

One day, in third grade, little Joseph Hateplum had a breakthrough. Out on the schoolyard he'd walked up to a little black first-grader and gave him the family bop on the top of the head. The little black kid had been reduced to tears and ran away. Fifteen other excited little boys crowded around Joseph to ask how he did it.

"I just walked up and bopped that damn import," said Joe.

All the surrounding little boys laughed.

This felt pretty good to Joseph Hateplum. And he set his sights on a new career. The KKK. He was leadership material.

He set fire to his first black kid when he was sixteen.

I found 22 floral lane, the entrance to a mobile home park where most of the trailers were run-down and rusty around the edges. Derelict cars and pickups lounged here and there, some with wheels some without. Mobile was a disappearing characteristic of this park.

I wondered as I approached the trailer door whether I should ask for Mr. Hateplum or just ask for the Grand High Wiz.

The screen door on the trailer hung askew on the hinge like a broken wing. I reached my hand through a tear in the nylon net and knocked on the metal door behind.

A heavy-faced woman in wiry dog curls opened the door and looked out. Her forehead and nose were flat, her jowls full, and the folds under her eyes so heavy I thought for a second she was wearing tea-bags.

"Excuse me, Mam. I'm looking for Joseph Hateplum?" I said cordially.

"You the FBI again?" she asked skeptically.

"No, no, I'm just an investigator," I corrected, "I'm on a case—"

"Undercover, huh?" said the woman, grunting with sour mirth, "My husband doesn't enjoy you undercover agents either."

"Mam, I'm not an agent and I'm not undercover."

"Only agents call me Mam around here. Everybody else calls me Sadie; except those that don't like me who calls me the Grand High Bitch..." Sadie looked to see how I took all this in.

I made my choice.

"Nice to meet you, Sadie," I said.

This was returned with a cautious nod.

"I just want to talk with your husband," I said.

"Well, you missed him. He went out early."

"Where?" I asked.

"He's down protesting at the school."

"Are they integrating the schools around here?" I asked with grave concern.

"No!," laughed Sadie, "He's down at the black school by the river. He's protesting that they *have* schools."

I shoulda knowed.

Chapter 61

I noticed several rambling orange school buses, like big bulbous beetles, driving along country roads as I drove down to the river. The rumbling vehicles were cheery to see in the morning. Most seemed packed with little shining black faces.

It wasn't hard to find the school. It turned out to be an elementary school with one crosswalk in front (there was only one road leading up to the place). Stationed at the crosswalk, a man dressed in white was leaning over the passing kids. Sewn to the chest of the man's white garb was an ornate Christian cross. Black kids in colorful clothing were walking hand in hand toward their school, but were stopping and hesitating before they reached the white man in the crosswalk.

What looked like a crossing guard was actually Joseph Hateplum.

It was an easy conclusion once you saw how he was harassing the kids. From where I parked, I watched the black children heading toward school. They were smiling, joking, and funny-minded as they walked together in little bunches. Clean faces and shining eyes. The happy unchallenging gazes of grade-schoolers still full of mischief and fun, walking in the early morning in a world that was yet fresh and clean.

But as they reached the crosswalk, Joseph Hateplum stepped forward to each little bunch and leaned down to say his magic words.

"Hey, you little niggers, what you need school for?"

I watched the smiling open kids' faces wilt.

I got out of my car and walked up to this figure in white. For a second, I felt that old "Wrath of God" come up, but I swallowed it back.

"Mr. Hateplum?" I said, interrupting the Grand High Wizard in his focus on the passing children.

"What?" challenged Joseph.

"I'm Morgan Hercules, a detective. Could I talk with you a few moments?"

"I'm busy. The answer is, maybe I did it, maybe I didn't."

"I need to ask you a few questions about the business of your organization. It concerns saving a life...You could help."

"Why should I do that?"

I shrugged. For the life of me, I didn't know why he would want to do that.

"Because it's a white person?" I said, inwardly cringing.

Joseph nodded.

"What do you want to know?"

"Back around 1987, you where just elected Grand High Wizard, right?"

"Yeah, we were doing pretty good in these parts then, too. We had maybe fifty sixty guys at the meetings."

"Did you receive any money, a great deal of money at that time?"

"We were doing pretty good. In fact, I remember one check came from somewhere called The Imperial Order of Watchers. It was a check for $500,000. We received it anonymously, with a letter saying we were to use it solely for the education of new KKK leaders. So we could get more of our people into higher political positions. We couldn't use it for nothing else. Or we'd be cut off, see? It was the beginning of a very bad period for my chapter."

"Outta here, don't come near me Blackie when I'm in the crosswalk!"

Joseph had screamed at a 3-foot boy with red and white striped shirt, black pants, and white socks who made the mistake of whistling as he crossed in the crosswalk. The little boy jump sideways and nearly fell on the seat of his pants.

"Why was receiving this money bad for the KKK?" I asked. As I looked around, I heard the rumble of an orange school bus coming down the road. The streams of walking black kids were moving well off the side of the road as the bus approached.

"Well, I did as the letter instructed, we pick out a whole cadre of future leaders of the KKK and used the money to send them to college. What a dumb move!"

"Why?"

"Well, after a couple years, they got good jobs and stopped coming to meetings."

"Who sent the checks?" I asked.

"The Imperial Order of the Watchers, that's all I know. The checks were good. We weren't supposed to find out. Klan secrecy."

I could see the big orange school bus now wheeling within twenty feet of us. It felt like it was coming on pretty fast, and I stepped back farther from the road.

Most accidents happen when you try to do two things at one time.

"Watch it!" I said.

Joseph, who had just stepped into the road and bent to curse at a black kid who'd successfully sneaked past him without being yelled at, at the same time raised and waved a hand to shush me for a moment.

He should have been watching out for the bus.

It flattened him like a pancake.

There was a big commotion on the bus as it lurched to a halt. Many school children wore frightened faces as I bent to look under the bumper, way underneath the bus, where the ex-leader of the KKK lay. He was definitely dead, the school bus engine still grunting over him. Fortunately, because he was wearing his KKK robe, it was easy to cover his face and wide-open eyes with the self-supplied sheet.

I got out from under the bus and then walked round and up into the side door to check with the driver.

A black woman in blue shorts, white shirt, and a blue cap, looked at me.

In a calm voice, she said, "Is he dead? Do I need to pull forward or backup any?"

The ghastly image of driving the bus back and forth over the dead man, as if just to make sure, hit me.

"No, you parked it there pretty good," I said.

"I always see him standing there yelling at these babies," said the driver to the windshield. "My brake foot just slipped."

I could see disappearing in this woman's face something I recognized: Morgan's Wrath of God. You don't mess with that.

"That's the way it goes," I said.

I told her to keep the kids in the bus and I would go call the police.

As I marched toward the school office, I strangely heard a song start flowing from the open bus windows. A child's voice, full of mocking, started with a slow rhythmic clapping but soon accelerated into a fast gospel reel.

"We shall overrun,

"We shall overrun,

"We shall overrun

"Toooo day..."

Chapter 62

Once back in San Francisco, I had Abdul report the happenings back in Alabama to Julie, as I unpacked the dirty clothes and repacked clean ones for my next little investigative trip. Julie sent a little handwritten note back with Abdul, implying in a fine curly feminine handwriting that we were getting nowhere fast.

Chapter 63

I had an odd dream that night before leaving town again. I dreamed I didn't know who the Emperor was and I didn't have a relationship with Julie.

It left me feeling a bit forlorn.

Both were true.

Chapter 64

I looked up from Abdul's background print outs, "So where does this Sergeant Voznesensky, leader of the First American Defense Brigade, hang out?"

"Black Peak, in Southern California. Just past Earp. It's in Arizona actually, Boss. It is right on the border. Overlooks the Colorado river."

"What's a survivalist group doing out there?"

"Just surviving, I suppose," replied Abdul.

I hoped to get more information about the Emperor from Sergeant Major Voznesensky than I did from Joseph Hateplum before he slipped under that bus.

According to Abdul's papers, Conrad Voznesensky had barely had a childhood. When he was six, his mother had died in a suicidal car accident. When the guard rail of a drawbridge had dropped in front of her, she'd got mad and jumped her car half-way across the river. Little Conrad's father, an ex-Marine corps sergeant, lay on the family couch drunk everyday. He died a year later, after turning orange like a pumpkin. Now completely abandoned, Conrad spent the rest of his childhood moving from foster home to foster home. Of course, he began to act out. In crowded foster homes, he began to organize little war parties that raided fruit trees and even neighbors' refrigerators. He fought with kids who had well-respected fathers. He blackened the eyes of Dr. John's son. He broke the nose of Mayor Bird's pride and joy. Foster homes began to check Conrad in and out like a library book.

Finally after high school, Voznesensky was allowed to join the Marines. He'd served in Korea. He did well. He declined an offer to enter officer's candidate school. He liked giving orders to squads and he liked getting his hands dirty. When he reupped for Viet Nam, he was a highly-regarded Sergeant Major, respected for his number of kills. Abdul had shown me Voznesensky wearing a Hawaiian lei of human ears.

He ran his teams with iron discipline, but was black spotted as having reached the top of his military capacities.

At 48, Voznesensky had retired. And suddenly abandoned and alone in America, he had nothing to do. Never a quitter, he'd gotten political enough to start the "Brigade," an armed survivalist group hidden in the treelines of Arizona.

I looked at the map, spread out in rectangular folds, the edges curled like corn husks. It was going to be a 12-hour drive at least, out into the desert, past Twenty-Nine Palms Marine base, old haunt of Sergeant Voznesensky, through the Sheep's Hole mountains, finally to Earp.

"How do I get to their compound after I get to Earp?" I asked.

"Mule, Boss," said Abdul.

"What?"

"Yes, the compound is fifteen miles off road, up on the mountain. Only way there is riding a mule."

"Great," I muttered. "Can't I just take a helicopter?"

Abdul shook his head gravely.

"Oh no, you don't want to be doing that. You know, the camp is full of Vet Nam vets. They are dredging up many hard feelings when hearing low-flying helicopters. You don't want to be providing target practice for small arms fire."

I grimaced and nodded.

I got in my old metallic green Camaro and took off the parking brake. The trunk was already packed with hiking gear. Next stop: Sergeant John Voznesensky, leader of the First American Defense Brigade.

As I drove off, I could see Abdul at the curb shouting at me his last advice about this heavily-armed, paramilitary group, the Brigade.

"And, Boss," I heard fading behind me, "Try not to scare them."

Chapter 65

My mule's name was Becky. I had arrived in Earp at 8 in the morning, and sure enough, as Abdul had said, a taciturn man had walked me behind the Shell station and pointed out Becky.

Becky's rental was $25 per day, but I could tell by the flies around her ears she was worth more.

"Guns?" asked the service station attendant. I suspected he might be a secret agent and doorman for the Brigade, though I didn't see any paramilitary give-aways on his oil-soaked overalls.

"No gun," I said.

The man nodded not believing me. "Well, if you have guns, they go in here, for the ride up."

The man pointed out a box tied with rope to the mule's side. It was a really big box.

"Anything bigger than a mortar, you have to rent another mule," warned the taciturn attendant. "The Brigade is always trying to slip them things by me. Tires old Becky out."

"Gotcha," I said. "No guns."

The man nodded not believing me.

The man pointed out across the river to the distant hills of Black Peak, elevation 1665 ft. "It's yonder, now git."

I didn't know if he was talking to me or the mule.

But Becky stepped off on her own.

Chapter 66

Fifteen miles on mule back is a painful experience. My legs felt like I was trying to carry a watermelon between my knees and still sit normally. Becky bobbed and plodded along, I believe half-dozing as she walked. We walked steadily for several hours past rocks, across a small bridge, planks really, over the Colorado, up into a treeline, finally, into the wooded canyons and bluffs of the mountain.

I saw no one, and smelled trees for the first time in years.

"Halt, Motherfucker, or I blow yer head off!"

The shout startled me, but Becky simply stopped and looked back calmly over her shoulder.

There stood a green-and-grey camouflaged young man, about 18, complete with flat top marine style cap. His face was scribbled with black and green war paint. He was hoisting an old M-1 carbine in my direction.

Becky broke wind with calm disdain.

Raising my hands over my head, I said, "Sorry about that."

Chapter 67

"State your business," said the camouflaged young man.

"I'm here to see Sergeant Voznesensky," I said.

"Guns?" asked the soldier.

I shook my head.

"Why not?" asked the soldier.

I shrugged. For a second we were both stumped.

"No guns today," I said, cheerfully.

"Okay, Voznesensky is up in compound Sheba. I gotta check to see if it's okay." He pulled up a small device with a stubby tail and spoke quietly into it. It chirped and crackled as he nodded and listened.

"What do you want?" said the soldier to me with new orders.

"I'm interested in the Brigade," I said.

The soldier nodded and spoke into his tailed box again. He nodded again.

"It's okay to go up," stated the guard militarily, "But stay on the trail, or I'm supposed to ace you."

"Okay," I said. Becky began to walk off again on her own. I hoped she knew enough to stay on the trail.

"You got any gum, candy, or anything?" called the camouflaged guard to me as an afterthought.

I hunched my shoulders apologetically.

"Sorry, no gun, no candy," I shouted back.

Chapter 68

Becky made her way up the canyon, and as I rode, I could see men carrying rifles walking along the cliffs and occasionally pointing down at me.

I tried to give a cheery wave.

Above the patrolling soldiers, I could see a lumber platform perched high in pine tree boughs, and from which a glass, either a rifle scope or sighting lens, panned left and right. I noticed prickly trails of barbed-wire, strung in tangled rolls, winding surreptitiously behind bushes up the hillside. I could also see small pie tins planted here and there, facing down hill at odd angles: Claymore mines. It made me feel just the slightest bit unwelcome.

Becky didn't mind. She just kept stepping up the cliff. She didn't care if a paramilitary brigade, suspicious and fully-armed, was looking down on her.

A greeting party of three soldierly-looking men, all unshaven, walked up and took Becky's reins. They said nary a word of greeting. They were dressed in the same green and grey camouflage of the earlier young guard, except these men were middle-aged, a bit paunchy, and a lot more sullen. Maybe it was just their many droopy pockets, filled with stuff like bullets, Swiss army knifes, and tumerous lumps which I took to be grenades. Maybe it was the bayonets and folded trench-diggers hanging at their belts. Maybe it was the swollen automatics, military 45's, hanging like workmen's tools on their hips. Whatever it was they looked mighty-well equipped for military sullenness.

A squared-shouldered man, crisply uniformed, stepped forward from a small gate in the compound fence. He was toting a heavy rifle that looked more like a pipe with a pistol grip, except that it had a workman's handle on top for carrying like a tool box. It was a big modernday military weapon without a bit of wood; the shoulder stock was simply an L with padding. Just looking at it made you feel like you might get snakebit. As the man looked over and spotted me, I saw a lightening bolt was stitched to his cap. He had grey temples and aggressive eagle-eyes, and he pointed a finger at me accusingly and said, "You're looking for Sergeant Major Voznesensky. And you found him, soldier. So shit your pants or say your business."

"Right," I said.

Sergeant Voznesensky's eyes narrowed, "Right what?"

"Right, Sergeant?" I queried, mustering the total of my military experience.

"Shit or say? Which?" said the Sergeant Major as a hint, skeptically tilting one eyebrow.

"Say," I said, comprehending.

At that time ever-reliable Becky took the opportunity to drop a horsey load, green and steaming in the trail.

The Sergeant took no notice.

"Good boy, come up here, and let's get a look at you."

Chapter 69

I got down off Becky and walked up into the compound. On entering the gate, I looked about. The encampment was filled with many lean-to shacks, lumber piles, and smoky campfires. Quite a few men were milling around, sitting on porches, cleaning guns, folding wrinkled wash. Chickens were strutting and scratching between shacks. I could hear chopping and shoveling, and orders shouted here and there in the distant trees. I could also hear the occasional pop-pop-pop of automatically gun fire used cautiously. The three middle-aged soldiers led Becky away toward a corral where ten to fifteen of her mule-kindred were standing. They were all standing stock-still, paying no attention to anything happening in the woodsy compound, their compass noses pointed determinedly at the empty hay troughs.

Sergeant Voznesensky now shook my hand.

"So son, why did you leave your comfy civilian bed and come all the way up here to join the First American Defense Brigade? Time to be a man among men?" Voznesensky's voice carried a momentary warmth.

"I guess not," I said.

"Well, if you're not here to defend Mother America from those wimped out, pansy-assed, scum-sucking, liberals bleeders, why exactly did you come?" he asked, his head ticking back and forth like a metronome to register his irritation.

"My name is Morgan Hercules," I said, "I'm a detective. I have a few questions."

"Did you ever serve?" asked the Sergeant.

"Sure," I said. I'd been in Cub Scouts and sold Clamorama tickets when I was a kid. But answering 'no' would be disastrous.

"I served a couple years in a small group in blue I can't talk about."

"Navy Seals?" asked the Sergeant.

I looked carefully through the Sergeant, signaling I indeed wouldn't talk about the top secret raids of the cub scouts.

"I have a question or two," I said. "It concerns the people I serve now. It concerns the life or death of an American woman. I'm looking into something that concerns a foreign criminal working here in the US. The Emperor. Have you had any contact with him?"

"Hell no. The Brigade wants to close the borders so hard the invaders leave their toes on the doorstep."

Give the Sergeant an A for picturesque speech.

"Sergeant Major, did you ever receive a large amount of funds sometime around 1987?"

The Sergeant looked at me. "You're trying to catch some foreign criminal?"

"It appears so," I said.

"Well, we did get a check in 1987. It was from a sister defense organization. The Empirical Order of American Defenders."

"How much?" I asked.

"One point two million. It gave me the money to buy up this mountainside and build the Brigade's headquarters here. Stock-pile weapons and modest quantities of munitions. We've got a little mine out back where we keep it buried. It's really what put the Brigade on the map."

"And the sister defense organization. You have close contacts?"

"No, never heard of them. But the money was good."

Just then two men walked slump-shouldered out of the bushes. Their uniforms looked as if they were suffering from a bad case of giant red measles. Both were sour-faced as they walked, red paint blotches plastered on their chests, faces, and hair.

"Looks like they lost the paint-ball war," I said. It always struck me funny that grown-men would run amok around the woods shooting gumballs of paint at each other.

"Naw," said the Sergeant, "That was an execution."

Voznesensky looked at me knowingly, "Too many discipline infractions."

Voznesensky whispered mirthfully, "It's good for moral. Especially the ones on the firing squad."

I drew my mouth into a knowing half-smile, half-grimace.

"Come with me, I want to show you something," Voznesensky said.

We took several steps toward the side of the camp which overlooked the canyon and the Colorado river. The Sergeant Major was swinging his rifle by its handle at his side like a paint bucket as he walked.

I nodded at the Sergeant's weapon.

116

"Nice gun," I said.

"That's not a gun," said Voznesensky in rebuff. "That's a fine .50 caliber Barrett M-82A1 recoil-operated semi-automatic, magazine-fed rifle. It has a 29 inch fluted Krieger barrel with muzzel brake, fires a 750 grain armor piercing projectile, muzzle velocity 2,800 feet per second. This Barrett is a battle-proven heavy sniper rifle great for 1,000 yard kills, packs enough wallop to shot through a buffalo lengthwise, or blow a man's head clear off, if you decide to punt."

"Huh. I thought it was a gun," I said blandly.

"It's a great sniper weapon. Especially in the forest. See, at the first shot, most gooks in an firefight take cover behind a tree for safety. They think they're safe behind ten to twenty inches of wood. Not so with this mother. I just shoot the trees."

Sergeant Voznesensky laughed at ancient jokes on his witless enemies.

"I thought the big boys just used napalm," I said.

"Willie Peter? Sure. But wc here in America, in the First American Defense Brigade, we have to put our own asses on the line. Everyone's got to pick up a gun and defend our democracy. We've got enough weak kneed, doped-out, momma-cunt lickers weakening the backbone of our country. Everybody, I mean everybody has to be ready to defend our country. That's what this Brigade is about. Every good general has to be willing to put the little people on the line, life or death, when it comes to winning the war against the enemy. And I'm the same. And I'll walk the wire, too. Barrett M-82 in hand."

"If we could just get these generals walking the front lines to wear red helmets and a sign that said *Shoot Me First*," I thought.

Chapter 70

I looked at Voznesensky's clenched jaw and eagle-eye, as he looked out over his mountain-side lair.

"Listen, son, what's out there is a threat to our freedom. My freedom and yours. What I see out there, in the weak-kneed liberal colleges, in the ghettos, the barrios, the bleeding liberal middle class, the gay parades, I see a lot of weak individuals. Momma's boys who want to be taken care of, who won't stand up and do anything for America. They just do namby pamby whatever they want. People just pursuing their own pursuits. It's a threat to our freedom. Anybody can push them around. What would we do if we were all like that? How would we fight a war? How would we raise strong defenses? If everybody were just individuals, namby pamby?"

"Son, you have to accept that we are abandoned here in America. You can't count on people to understand you and support you. America is the land of the helpless and lost. You have to stand alone against that! Face it, you are abandoned."

"Oh, oh," I thought, "we've reached childhood. We'll be talking about Dad and Mom next."

"And you know two of my pet peeves?" said Sergeant Voznesensky suddenly to me, "Drunks and bungee jumpers!"

I nodded as seriously as I could.

"We have to be strong against these weak-sisters. It requires discipline, and pretty sturdy discipline, just to keep organized against them. They don't care about you or me. You are pretty well abandoned in this life. You can't let it overwhelm you. You have to defend against it. You can't let down. The world is filled with people who don't care, wouldn't help you if you were in trouble. The only thing you can do about it is get organized, get tough, and prepare to fight. You think any brigade of love-chanting hippie-freaks is going to take this hill from me?"

I remarked that I hadn't heard the term hippie-freak in years. The Sergeant was more than quaintly out of touch.

"No, somebody wants something from me, I just pull out the Barrett M82 an tell them to suck this."

I listened to Voznesensky's rant. He was pretty mad at somebody. But he didn't know who. I sensed deep in him a secret fear, an inner helplessness against those he felt surrounded by. He was worried about a deep inability to affect others, other than in the clearest most absolutely delineated lines, the lines of military command. The enemy out there, they were the weak, the non-fighters, the liberals, the educated, the non-military, the unorganized, and of course, Mom and Dad. And when you had an enemy you couldn't deal with, it called for retreat and fortification with arms.

Especially if it was an unconscious enemy within.

"So join the Brigade, son," Voznesensky coaxed. "It'll do you good."

"Sure," I thought, "Like a flower pot on the head."

I thankfully declined.

Chapter 71

I asked the Sergeant a few more questions concerning the money that he had used to found his organization. But it was evident, it had been a windfall from heaven, and he'd taken it without question to fulfill a dream, his own self-bought army, aimed at the enemies of choice.

Standing at cliff edge, the Sergeant then regaled me with a hurtful picture of the rotting marrow and stinking guts of America, something he meant to right. He pointed out across the canyon, the forest below, the winding river, to the distant blue mountains.

"When they come, we'll be ready. We won't have forgotten how to fight. We'll be standing tall, like our revolutionary forefathers. And we'll be armed to the teeth. And by God, we'll be ready for them."

Voznesensky turned his fiery eagle-eye on me.

"Who's them?" I asked.

Stabbing his hand at the golden horizon, Voznesensky blurted, "Them...them...the enemy!"

"Sergeant," I said, "that's California."

Chapter 72

Becky was summarily fetched for me, and I was sent on my way back down the mountain side. I was glad to be getting away from that rat pack.

As I descended, I thought about the Brigade and its secret fund. I had every suspicion that they had received their money from the Emperor.

I was also getting suspicions about the nature of the Emperor's handiwork.

Hateplum had received money to fund the education of leaders in the KKK. It eventually led to desertions and the demise of that little group.

Here, the Emperor's money had funded the building of the First American Defense Brigade headquarters. Voznesensky had purchased an isolated patch of land and built primitive living conditions at best. He'd packed up his little band of paramilitarians and went to live voluntarily behind protective fences and barbed wire, walked by armed guards. They had little contact with their surrounding neighbors. They lived a stiff military regime. They were fulfilling the Sergeant's vision of preparedness, as they lived within the confines of their First American Defense Brigade dream.

Looking back up the mountainside as Becky trotted happily back to her home gas-station and feedbag, I looked at the receding militant's compound, funded by the Emperor.

It was essentially a prison.

Chapter 73

Emperor's comment

So I am either a fool, a cynic, or a bloody genius. You can throw open the window, but who can throw out the baby? You should be writing this down.

Chapter 74

Sometimes, of course, I feel sorry for certain types of criminals. The really unconscious ones that got into trouble, for whom for some reason the light just never blinked on.

You know, like Anna Tortmen, a long-suffering unmarried 350-pound woman, 31 years old, who had a 68-year-old man say something about her that offended her and so she knocked him down in the park and throttled the old guy till he was dead. Then she got on a bus and went home and waited for the police. She remarked later the old guy kinda reminded her of her father of whom she was deathly afraid and who had always called her "elephant-girl."

Or Kevin Stillboy, 12-year-old child murderer.

Red-haired, freckled-faced, thick glasses, Kevin was a quiet but kind of slow kid. He had a Dad who had an explosive temper, the kind that threw your toys against the wall, breaking them, if you didn't clean up your room. The strict father who squashed protest with real belligerence. Kevin's mother, passive, only offered the insistent logic of Kevin's failures and the need for correction.

So Kevin had a stutter.

His older sister was ashamed of him. She avoided Kevin and yelled at him to stay away from her at home and school.

Children at school made fun of him, ragged him till he hung around the outer cyclone fences by himself.

He played only with the smaller kids.

One day, Kevin was playing in the vacant lot with his little neighbor friend, 5-year-old Joey who liked to hang around the older Kevin.

A black car was parked beside the lot. Kevin and Joey went over to look in the windows. An insurance agent, walking back from a local house call, yelled at the kids to get away from his car.

Kevin and little Joey stepped back and stood as the agent approached with his brief case. It was hot, the agent sweating, his forehead greased like a basted turkey.

"What are ya doing round my car?" yelled the agent.

Little Joey shrugs.

Kevin says, "Nuh, nuh, nuh..nuthin."

Irritated, (he'd just lost a sale), insurance agent sneers, "Nuh, nuh, nuthin? Get out of here you little stuttering asshole."

He gets in the car, slams the door, and drives off.

Kevin and Joey run back to the vacant lot.

Joey trips, falls, and starts crying because he's hurt his leg.

Kevin looks down on the crying Joey.

He looks and he gets tense.

He goes over, picks up a heavy rock, hefts it up, and smashes Joey in the head.

He later tells police it was because Joey, crying, seemed so little and helpless. He just got really mad.

I, Morgan Hercules, recognize this: it is the sick side of the Wrath of God.

So you be the detective: Who killed Joey?

A. Kevin

B. Insurance Agent

C. Explosive-tempered Father

D. Rational unfeeling Mother

E. Shamed Sister

F. Cruel school children

G. All of the above

It wasn't hard to solve these cases.

Chapter 75

Emperor's comment:

Would there be jails large enough to hold all of us?

Chapter 76

I was just finishing up reviewing my notes when Abdul walked into the office carrying a flimsy sheet of paper.

"Boss, look at this."

"What is it?" I asked.

"It's an FBI dispatch, faxed this morning."

I winced to find Abdul so deeply involved in intercepting FBI data.

"It says here there was an attack and kidnapping attempt on Sergeant Voznesensky and the Brigade."

"What?" I said.

Abdul quickly reported that the Sergeant had taken a small squad outside the compound to hunt for survivalist food. I assumed that meant berries and insect grubs.

Automatic weapons fire started blasting around them. Five of Voznesensky's men dropped dead in the first fusillade. Voznesensky took shelter behind a rock. Men in blue jackets with governmental DEA letters on their backs wiped out his entire squad. Voznesensky, alone, returned fire.

It was then the attackers made their mistake. They bedded down behind trees waiting for Voznesensky to run out of ammunition.

Voznesensky cranked a cartridge into his Barrett M-82 and started shooting junipers for all he was worth.

He killed five men with five shots.

This raised some warranted consternation among the attackers and the remaining blue jackets abandoned their trees and retreated fast.

The police, FBI, and press corps arrived by helicopter within the hour. A quarter mile off, they hung cautiously in the air and asked by loudspeaker for permission to land.

Voznesensky was joyous. He had to be restrained from taking ears.

But those who lived with Voznesensky looked at the dead packed up in body bags and their faces were grim. This included the mules.

The dead in blue jackets had no identification papers and were definitely not government agents. (I'm sure the director of the FBI blew a big sigh of relief.)

Finger prints were being taken from stiff trigger fingers.

I thought back to the attempted kidnapping of Mother Teresa.

"Abdul," I said, "I get the feeling we're being followed."

Chapter 77

The telephone rang like an addled woodpecker rattling my metal bedpost. I opened my eyes and saw black. Then the clock came into focus: it was 3 am.

"Yallo?" I said, then cleared my throat, "What do you want?"

It was Julie breathless and excited.

"Morgan?"

"It's me," I said yawning.

"I just got a phone call, it was really strange. A voice just said 'If you're looking for the Emperor, Willie the Sneak is at the Bridgeport Hotel.' Then he hung up."

"Okay," I said.

"Who's Willie the Sneak?" asked Julie.

"He's a guy was trying to sell information about the Emperor."

"So are you going to talk to him right now?" asked Julie.

"Hmmm," I said, which either meant I was or I wasn't.

"Why not?" asked Julie, assuming I wasn't.

"My pajamas," I said.

"What about your pajamas?" asked Julie, exasperated.

"Because," I said still groggy, "people laugh at me when I run into a hotel lobby in my pajamas."

"Take them off!"

"Julie, we don't want to make anybody sick."

"Morgan! Are you going?!"

"Yeah, yeah," I said. I knew I'd be going all along, but I just felt like a little 3 am repartee.

Chapter 78

I dialed Abdul's number. The phone rang, the receiver lifted.

"Yeah, Boss?" came Abdul's sleepy voice.

"How'd you know it was me?" I asked.

"Boss, not even the tenants in my building call me at 3 am," said Abdul.

"Julie got an anonymous call. Willie the Sneak is in the Bridgeport. Can you find out which room?" I asked.

Abdul's voice perked up, "Yeah, yeah, I'm having it for you in one second. Good, Boss, we need to see him."

The phone went dead.

Then it rang two minutes later.

"Boss?" said Abdul.

"Yeah," I said.

"Willie the Sneak is in Room 204."

"How'd you find out so soon?"

"I just called room service and asked to confirm which room had a man named Willie signing his checks. They said Mister Cheese sandwiches is in 204. Evidently he has a cheese sandwich every night."

If figured, Willie, the criminal rat, was having his nightly cheese and crusts.

Chapter 79

In spite of Julie's imprecations, I doubted anyone named "Willie the Sneak" would invite me into his room in the black A.M. So I waited to go call on him first thing that morning. I slept while I waited.

I got to the Bridgeport while the doorman in red riding jacket was still hosing down the sidewalk. Willie the Sneak was residing in quaint old digs. The Bridgeport, with its revolving glass door and Mediterranean carpets wasn't the highest quality downtown hotel, but it was holding up well, like San Francisco Madams of yore.

I went into the lobby, nodded at a sleepy looking deskclerk resting on his elbows at the front desk, and sat down in a chair beside the house phone.

I dialed 204.

"Hello?" came a worried voice.

"Willie?" I asked.

"Who wants to know?" was the cautious reply.

"I hear you have some information to sell. About the Emperor. I'm very interested."

"Finally," said the voice. Then with sudden caution, "How did you find me?"

"Someone called a woman I know," I said.

"A Julie Veingold?" said Willie.

"Yeah," I said.

"I called her," said Willie. "I have some information about the Emperor she might want to buy."

"Maybe we're buying, depends on the information."

"Who are you?" asked Willie.

"A detective serving Julie."

"Are you with anyone?"

"What?" I said.

"You represent anybody else? Who's buying?"

"Just me," I said.

"Who is that?" asked Willie.

"Morgan Hercules," I said.

"You with the Emperor? I never heard of you."

"No, I'm not with the Emperor."

"So why are you trying to locate him?" Willie asked.

"It's for his daughter," I said.

"Ah," said Willie. "I got information. But it'll cost you a mighty big buck."

"Can do," I said.

"You're not with those cheapskates the FBI? Goddamn bunch of check bouncers."

"Cash," I said, "If we come to terms, and you've got real information."

There was a silence as Willie the Sneak thought things out. I could tell he didn't know me, but he also wanted money the envious way a starving rat wants cheese laid carefully on the trigger of a rat trap.

"Okay, okay. Let's meet," Willie said deciding.

"Where, when?" I asked.

"The alley behind the Bridgeport hotel, at 9:00 am."

I looked at my watch, I'd have coffee for a half-hour at the hotel cafe, then walk out the back door.

"See you soon," I said.

Chapter 80

I called Abdul just to check in.

"I found him," I said.

"Good, Boss, what did he say?"

"I'm meeting him in the alley behind the Bridgeport in a half-hour. He didn't say much. He's very interested in selling information about the Emperor."

"What information?"

"I don't know."

"Has he talked to anyone else, Boss?"

"He mentioned the FBI. Actually he said 'those check bouncers.'"

"Call me back, Boss, if you find out more." The phone went dead.

I looked at the phone. I felt like I'd been summarily dismissed by my own office slave.

Chapter 81

I stepped out the backdoor of the Bridgeport and looked up and down the alley. It was a narrow brick canyon. At one end, about a block away, I could see several men beside a big van, unloading coffin size boxes, and laying them in a wall that blocked the alley. Down the opposite direction, I could see several cars parked nose to the wall, blocking the other end of the alley, with three or four men slouching against them drinking from paper bags. Across from me stood a big metal trash container, half the size of a dump truck. It was navy blue, with two heavy lids raised up on top, like the jaw of a huge trap ready to slam down. Hunched down beside the dumpster, in its shadow, squatted a man looking very nervous.

I could only guess this was Willie the Sneak.

I walked over to the trash bin. The man squatting beside it eyed me carefully without saying a word. He had beady eyes, a long nose with a sneering mouth underneath, and two front teeth that looked ideal for taking the caps off bottles.

"Willie?" I said.

Willie squirmed a bit before he answered.

"You alone?" he asked in a surprisingly high voice, almost the squeak of a pinched balloon.

"Yeah, I talked to you earlier."

"I've got information that that Julie will be very interested in."

"What's that?" I said.

"I have information about who her father is," said Willie.

"What's that? That her father may be the Emperor?" I asked.

"How did you know?!" cried Willie, taken aback.

"Is that the information you were going to sell us?" I asked.

"Yeah," said Willie.

"We already knew it," I said. "How did you find out?"

"I did some work for the Emperor in Europe, I never met him. No one has ever seen him. But I was in his office once. I stole something from his bulletin board. And I got a list of people that he sent money to. From a trash bin."

"Worked for the Emperor, but you never saw him?"

"Right, I was just a kind of money runner. I only ever met one little brown guy who delivered envelopes to me and then I'd take'm here to the states. If you want to know more, it's going to cost you big bucks."

"So it sounds like we already know all your information. What should we pay for?" I said.

"Come on," said Willie.

I looked up and down the alley. The men down at the van were now opening the boxes with crowbars. The men drinking from paper bags at the other end were opening the car doors and pulling out long objects that looked like brooms wrapped in cloth.

"Here, I'll show you what I stole from the Emperor's office. But it'll cost you two thousand bucks. Cash."

"Sure," I said. Why not.

Willie slowly stood up; not surprisingly his head stopped rising at my breast pocket. Willie was fumbling inside his pants pocket.

"This is it," said Willie with defiance, "And I want the money this afternoon."

I wasn't too impressed with Willie's business acumen. I took the piece of paper he'd handed me. It was a sheet of cheap tablet paper with specks of wood pulp and heavy blue lines, the kind found in elementary schools. One side was nearly blank, except for a poorly lettered street address, written in a child's blockish handwriting. It looked as if a kid had been pretending to address an envelope, having trouble keeping the lines going straight. The address was to Julie's apartment.

On the other side of the paper was a child's drawing:

It seemed to be a picture of a kid playing in a pile of money.

"See, it's a drawing by the Emperor's kid," said Willie. "It proves she's related. Why else would he keep it."

"Why's this worth anything?" I asked.

"You know the Emperor's daughter, you can grab her, shake some big money out of the Emperor..." Willie's beady eyes narrowed and did a sneering smile.

"I'd expect it would be worth it to the daughter to have that back," said Willie. "Two thousand bucks, and I don't tell nothing."

Except he'd probably already told everyone he could think of.

"Okay," I said, folding the paper and putting it in my pocket.

Then World War III broke out.

Chapter 82

Three tremendous hammer blows slammed the garbage bin above Willie's head, followed by the loud report of guns down the alley.

The surprise knocked me back. I slammed my spine to the wall across the alley as Willie went to his knees in fear.

The men by the van were now in prone positions on their boxes, militarily firing AK-47s our way.

Bang bang bang bang bang bang. Wack! Wack! Wack! Wack!

The gunfire was smacking hell out of the metal bin behind Willie.

"Get down!" I shouted to Willie. It should have been me getting down, because I could see Willie fast flattening on the pavement like an obedient rug.

Then gunfire erupted from the other end of the alley. I looked and the men with the brooms were now all business firing M-16s.

Bang bang bang bang bang! Wack! Ping! Wack!

I was holding my breath, an easy target. The garbage bin, with the heavy lid still up, was doing a shuttering jig.

Then I noticed splinters flying around the men on the crates. It looked like they were under fire, and indeed, one man dropped his weapon and rolled off the box, clearly shot. No more bullets were whacking the garbage bin around Willie as the group by the van retrained their sights on the other group firing from cars at the far end of the alley.

Both sides opened up on each other in earnest. The noise was deafening.

Bullets were whizzing left and right. I could actually hear them whipping by like angry bees. I thought of the hotel door behind me, but realized I'd have to lean into the alley to pull it open, making me more of a target. I sank to a huddled squat.

"I should be dead by now" popped into my head. Inspiring thought as usual.

I looked down the alley at the attackers by the van. A tailgate was lowering; revealed behind it was a man in black manning a 50-caliber machine gun.

I heard Willie whine in anticipation.

These customers meant business.

The machine gun opened up with a roar, punching fist-size holes in the cars at the other end of the alley. The little band behind the cars ducked for cover.

Willie seeing for an instant that he was no longer the prime target, seized the moment to scramble up and into the blue garbage bin.

Then a man behind one of the cars popped up long enough to aim a short stick back down the alley.

"Christ, a grenade launcher," I thought.

There was a light pop. The van with the machine gun exploded.

I covered my face with my arms as metal and wood pieces, and one body, did a graceful arch and swan dive toward me.

There was a temporary lull as both sides took in the fact that the grenade launcher had scored a bullseye.

Willie's head popped up over the edge of the garbage bin. He leaned out, looking down the alley at the strewn metal and dazed figures with guns.

He should have been looking up.

The ponderous lid of the trash bin slammed down.

I have to admit it was as clean a kill.

Willie made a squeaky wheeze, then hung limp. That garbage bin lid had come down hard on his neck.

No doubt about it: in death, Willie had been ratified.

As if on command, all the gunfire ceased. I took the moment to tear open the hotel backdoor, throw myself through, and run.

Chapter 83

Wow. Somebody really didn't like Willie the Sneak.

Chapter 84

Emperor's comment:

Poor Willie. When I sent my men, I really didn't mean to kill him. Quite the opposite, really. My merry band of highly-trained commandos was hired and instructed to take Willie alive at all costs. They just encountered trouble. They couldn't help it if Willie chose to hide in a killer garbage can. Really.

Chapter 85

A bit jittery, I drove fast winding my way back to my office via several side streets, checking to see if I was followed.

I thought a bit about my meeting with Willie and the ensuing firefight. First, it meant there were at least two groups after Willie and perhaps myself. We definitely had two teams firing on each other. Considering the small amount of time between my setting up a meeting with Willie and our alley ambush, it also meant that whoever was following was following pretty close.

I was going to have to be careful about how I gathered information.

Chapter 86

"It's our address, but I didn't draw this," said Julie, her monocle dropping from her eye. She looked up winking at me to get things back into focus. The child's drawing that Willie had handed me was spread before her on the kitchen table.

Abdul was looking grave and disappointed to find that Willie had been killed in the alley before I'd found out more.

"He didn't say who he'd talked to about this?" asked Abdul. "That could give us some clues..."

"We had two groups," I shrugged, "and no love lost between."

"I imagine one group was from the Emperor," said Julie resignedly.

I could see she was getting a grim realization about who her criminal father was. It was a tough window to open.

Just then a lumbering figure in blue flannel nightgown walked into the kitchen.

It was Julie's sister, Anna Elisabeth. Round-faced, pale, and ever-smiling, she was carrying an empty cup in her hand, heading for the sink. She nodded hello. At the sink, she poured water in her cup. She nodded hello again as she returned across the kitchen.

As she passed Julie, she looked down on the drawing on the kitchen table. Her eyes lit and smiling she picked up the picture. Without a word she folded the paper, put it in her night gown pocket, and left the room.

I realized who the Emperor's daughter was.

Chapter 87

That night the newspapers reported a spate of gunfire in an alley behind the Bridgeport hotel. It was attributed to gang violence. No bodies were found, except that of a man dead in a dumpster. Police were not sure if he was involved, it looked more like another accidental death. The police were not overly concerned: gang violence was gang violence,(even if it involved a 50-caliber machine-gun and grenade launcher.) I was once told by a Potrero Hill cop that without an actual person down they sometimes didn't even bother with a "shots-fired" call. You've got to pick the crimes you can mend. And spend a lot of time cleaning up the garbage after.

It was reported that the victim, who had died of a broken neck in the dumpster, was one Willard Raton Sneakleman.

Ah, Destiny.

Chapter 88

The next day, I wanted to see if I could find some other directions to go in. I called Julie and asked if she'd have lunch with me. She said yes. My heart was gladdened.

Julie met me at a little cafe off Union square, the kind where you carry a tray from a counter to the table. And where there's always an old woman in a ski-cap eating soup in the corner.

Julie looked her beautiful self.

"Thanks for coming," I said as we sat with our trays.

"Why so formal, Morgan?" asked Julie.

"I guess this is just a business meeting," I said.

"Just?" asked Julie.

I blinked. She'd caught me. Damn smart people, always reading between the lines.

"Okay, I like you, Julie," I said, "There's no doubt about it. Please don't burn me at the stake or anything for it. I like you and I want to help. Okay?"

"Thank you, Morgan," said Julie. "I appreciate it. But I mainly need the help? You know?"

"Sure," I said. I tried not to sound like I just swallowed an elephant of disappointment.

We both lifted a few spoons of soup in silence.

"We don't seem to be making much progress," said Julie.

"We're making progress," I said.

"How is that?" Julie asked.

"We've talked to 3 people on our list. We know who doesn't know anything."

"I think three times zero equals zero," said Julie.

"No, Julie, we're making progress, we're eliminating possibilities. Don't be a doubting mother to her son. We need the confidence to keep going."

"I wouldn't know that, I never really had a mother," said Julie.

"Yes, I know, you live in a kind of quiet world, in a distant galaxy, on the planet Psychologica Archeologica."

"No fair!" said Julie."You have to admit, my homelife was different from yours."

"I don't seem to know a whole lot about it, and maybe you don't either," I said. I realized I was a little peeved. I realized it was probably from swallowing down that elephant.

"Sorry," I said, "I didn't mean it."

Julie nodded. She looked at me intently.

"Morgan, what was your mother like?" Julie asked.

"My mother? A busy woman, a little distant, I think it might a been a kind of cold household," I said.

"Well, then accept that my mother was very distant, and it was a very cold household. Understand that part of me, can you?" said Julie.

"Sure," I said. "I understand."

"Except," I continued.

"Except what?" asked Julie.

"Except, you still choose to live there."

Chapter 89

"Look, Morgan, do you have some questions for me?" asked Julie with a touch of consternation.

"Yes, I'd like to check a little into your background. Abdul came up with surprisingly little. Only your birth certificate, and school documents."

"Do you have anything else for me to go on? Letters from relatives, old trunks of stuff?" I asked.

"No," said Julie.

"Morgan, admit you're stumped," said Julie.

"No! We know the Emperor is out there. I'm finding traces. I'll keep looking until I find him," I said.

"Clueless," laughed Julie.

"Looking for clues," I replied. I had my own sense of pride.

"Well, good for you Mister Detective," said Julie. "At least there's one thing I like about you."

"What's that?" I said, my ears pricking up, "My gallant chin, my heroic nose?"

"You slavish spirit," said Julie. She patted me on the back of my hand. "I thank you for it."

I shrugged.

"I'll remember that."

Chapter 90

"Dr. Pushkin?" I said, hoping I had the right old man. It had taken me several phone calls from the quiet of my home to three local hospitals until I was able to get a number for the retired physician.

"Yes, how may I help you?" came a wavering old voice.

"Dr. Pushkin, my name is Morgan Hercules. I'm a private investigator here in San Francisco."

There was a suspicious silence on the other end of the line, so I hurried on.

"I'm trying to locate someone that you may have met a long time ago. It involves the birth of a Julie Veingold. You were the physician at the birth, back in 1970."

"Veingold? 1970? That's way back there, partner."

"I'm trying to locate her parents..." I said.

"Hmmm," said the Doctor. I could sense him relax now that it was an apparent lineage question.

"I have a copy of the birth certificate here before me," I said. It doesn't list the father, nor the mother's full name. Just Veingold. I was wondering if you remembered anything more."

"Can you hold on a minute, I have my file cabinets in a back room here. I can check it, if you like."

"Please," I said.

In about five minutes Dr. Pushkin came back on the line. A note of enthusiasm had entered his voice as I could tell he was getting into taking part in a detective case.

"Yes, I have it here," he said. "Julie Veingold. Born 1970."

"No listing of the father's name?" I asked.

There was a brief pause. "No, UA means 'unavailable'. Or "usual asshole" as I think of it in these unwed mother things."

The Doctor paused.

"You know, I remember the birth now. I was concerned about the mother."

"Why was that?" I asked.

"Oh, I wasn't sure whether I could communicate instructions to her when it came time to push. I remember she was a young Down syndrome woman. I'd never delivered for such a person before. I was pretty concerned. But the baby came out fine. A beautiful squalling baby, completely normal. I suggested the baby should be given immediately to a foster home. I was uncertain that the newborn could be taken care of adequately by the mother, being retarded and all."

"Do you remember anything more about the name of the mother?" I asked, "The copy just says Vcingold here."

"Well, no, an older woman had just brought the mother into my office in an emergency. My copy has the mother's name as A. E. Veingold."

"A. E." I said, stunned.

Chapter 91

"Julie?" I said cautiously over the phone.

"Hello? That you Morgan?" answered Julie. "Have you found something out, perchance?"

"Yes, can I come over and talk with you?"

"Sure, come over."

"Be right there," I said. I put down the phone and took a deep breath. Sometimes that steadied me when I was the bearer of bad news.

Chapter 92

I entered the apartment building. I walked past Abdul's door with the "Abdul Dallah, Concierge Extraordinaire" sign and up the stairs to Julie's apartment.

Julie opened the door with a half-smile. She was wearing a beehive of red curlers and a pink bathrobe thick as a throw rug.

"Don't mind me, I'm just getting ready for a lecture," smiled Julie. "I'm discussing the myth of the concept of 'throwbacks' in industrial society. You know, the fear that an educated mother would suddenly have a chimp for a kid."

I nodded and grimaced.

"What is it, Morgan?" Julie said, concerned.

"Oh, I need to talk with you about something I found out," I said. "Can we sit down?"

"Sure." Julie motioned me to the deep purple couch, the velour soft as a cat's fur.

"Morgan, I have a Ph.D.," she said, "I think you can talk without worrying about whether I can take it."

"You know, Julie," I started, "When you investigate, sometimes you find out things you don't expect. It's like throwing open a window, and you look out. You sometimes see the thing you're looking for, and sometimes you see other unexpected things. But if you look out and see the whole picture, you may see beautiful things you didn't know about, and things you don't like, but if you see the whole pictures it's safer and you're better prepared..."

"Morgan, I suspect all this philosophical drivel about windows is leading up to bad news. Can we get to that?" asked Julie. If she'd had her monocle, I'm sure she would have affixed it on her face and trained it on me like a gunsight.

I nodded.

"Julie, you aren't the Emperor's daughter," I said.

"You mean this was all a mean hoax?"

"No," I said, shaking my head, "Anna Elisabeth is the Emperor's daughter."

"Then how can I not be the Emperor's daughter, too?"

"Julie, you are the Emperor's granddaughter."

Julie's eyebrows were in a perplexed snarl. She looked ravishing even when totally confused.

"Spit it out, Morgan, what point are you making?" said Julie.

"Julie, Anna Elisabeth is your mother."

Chapter 93

Julie sat in complete silence for nearly a minute.

I sat watching her face go through a series of emotions. I saw consternation, bewilderment, pain, incredulous shock. Then I saw more shock. Julie's eyes closed tightly. Finally when they came up, she looked at the far wall where hung the lavish false portrait of her mother, complete with little tiara. Then her gaze traveled across the room to the closed door of sick Anna Elisabeth.

"Ha, and me about to go give a lecture about throwbacks," said Julie grimly to the air before her. I could see her face was about to crumple.

"Well, Julie, this makes you kind of a throw-forward..." I said, striving as hard as I could to say something truly lame.

"Excuse me," said Julie.

She went into her own room and closed the door.

Chapter 94

This wasn't the first time I'd jerked a rug out from underneath a person's feet.

I knew you couldn't help the person up right away. You had to let them lie there in a heap for a while.

I decided to return to my office and wait for her call.

Chapter 95

A half hour later in my office the phone rang.

"Are you sure?" said the distant voice.

"Yes, Julie," I said.

The phone clicked dead.

Chapter 96

"Hello?" I said into the phone.

"She can't be my mother! Morgan, you've got it wrong, as usual!"

"Julie, I did some checking. I talked with the attending physician. In 1970 a Down syndrome woman named A.E. Veingold gave birth to a Julie Veingold. The Doctor remembers it well. It's uncommon. I haven't made a mistake, Julie."

"Well, there's no reason to gloat about it!" she screamed into the phone.

After the click, I put the receiver back in the cradle.

Chapter 97

"Yes, Julie?" I said picking up the phone.

"Morgan, Morgan, I just can't think of her as my mother. I can't, oh!"

I heard weeping on the other end of the line.

"I'll be right over," I said.

Chapter 98

When Julie opened the door she was no longer in bathrobe and curlers, but now was in a prim blue dress with small white polka dots. Her eyes were puffy and red, her hands jittery and she seemed to have no place to put them. Her attempt at smiling at me was disappointing.

Without a word she waved me into the living room.

I seated myself back on the purple couch.

Julie swallowed. "Thank you, Morgan for coming back over. I'm sorry I yelled—"

"Don't worry about it," I interrupted.

Julie sat in the overstuffed chair beside the couch. She crossed her legs and looked off in the other direction.

"What am I to do? Anna is my sister. Not my mother!" Julie said.

"I've accepted her as my sister so long. I don't seem able to think of her as my mother. Morgan, I can't..." Julie's lower lip trembled.

"It's okay, Julie," I said, "You don't have to. Think of her as anything you want."

"But I need ...I need to have someone...you can't ignore where you come from..."

"Well, no," I said, nodding my affirmation.

"Morgan, how can I come from there? How?" burst Julie, "My mother, I thought she was this other person in the painting. I realize now I'd worked my whole life to be like her. To build myself in her image. I got my PH. D. because I wanted to be smart like her. I wanted to succeed like her. I wanted to be looked up to, and approved of by her. I realize I worked my whole life, so hard, to fit myself into the shadow of my mother's image. But now I find I'm the daughter of someone else. Who's slow. Who smiles at nothing. Who can't read. How can I be the child of a woman who can't spell my name?"

Julie jumped up from her overstuff chair and paced a few steps, shaking her hands as if they were wet.

"Morgan, I'm the daughter of someone who's retarded! A fat head!" exclaimed Julie into the air toward the ceiling. "All the cruel words ever used for Anna."

"You are," I said, "so what?"

"Well, then, who am I now?"

"Julie, maybe you're free to be yourself." I said. I hunched my shoulders. "Just yourself, that's all."

Chapter 99

Just then Anna Elisabeth's door opened a crack, and an eye appeared looking out. It hesitated there behind the door, uncertain whether to come out among the two brooding adults.

"Anna," said Julie, working at smiling, "It's okay, come on out."

You could tell Anna didn't have a clue what was going on. Only some kind of radar let her read the heavy feelings emanating in the room and feel the misgivings clouded up there.

Anna, wearing the same heavy pink bathrobe Julie had had on earlier, waddled into the room, a bit hunchbacked, ape-ish, blinking and smiling. She went directly over and threw her arms around Julie.

Julie's smile turned grim. Then she slowly put her arms around Anna Elisabeth's shoulders.

"Poor, Anna," said Julie, "Nobody knows who you are either."

Julie hugged her mother as she cried.

Chapter 100

Julie and I had coffee in the kitchen. Julie's visage was still morose. Anna had wandered off somewhere else in the apartment.

"You still have your grandfather, we can find him," I said.

"The so-called Emperor," sneered Julie, "Just what I need, a criminal ancestor who demolishes the economies of small countries. Wonderful."

I sipped my coffee.

Julie made an animated mock introduction, "And I'd like you to meet Julie, her grandfather single-handedly turned all the Belgian and Danish children into beggars temporarily..."

"You've got a point," I said.

"Damn right," said Julie.

"But Anna, your mother, is still sick," I said, "Do you want to carry on?"

Julie's beautifully shaped eyebrows furrowed into a V.

She sat for several seconds frowning.

"Yes, we still have to find the Emperor."

I nodded. Not off the hook yet. I could also tell that Julie now wanted to give him a piece of her mind.

"I'll get on it," I said.

"And, Morgan," said Julie firmly, "I'm going with you."

Chapter 101

Protest as hard as I could, I couldn't dissuade Julie from joining Abdul and me on our quest for the Emperor.

I said it'd be dangerous.

She said that if I was her servant, and it was dangerous, she had to share the danger.

I said she didn't know anything about investigations.

She said she had a Ph.D. in Psychological Archaeology, she was a researcher, an investigator, mind you.

"Who's next on your list?" Julie asked.

"Dr. Billie Kookie, Dr. Needler, and Charles Ashe," I said unhappily.

"Good, those fools are just my kind of meat," said Julie.

"You're not going," I said, pronouncing my last word.

"Am," said Julie, edging in her own.

Chapter 102

Back in the office, I'd told Abdul that Julie was joining our investigations.

"Boss, that is a terrifically bad idea!" he said. "You can't be letting her do this."

I then told Abdul the sobering news that I'd done some checking into Julie's birth and discovered who Julie's real mother was.

"What?" shouted Abdul. His face went red. He looked truly angry, an Indian pug dog, riled to bark.

"Easy, Abdul. It's shaken the roots of her world," I said. "That son-of-a-bitch Emperor set her up for this. And it's a bitter plum to swallow. Julie's choking on it. And if we don't let her do something, she just may not swallow it and go on. If you want to be angry, be angry at this damned Emperor. It's just a situation. And now Julie's unfortunately part."

"You couldn't talk her out of it?"

I shook my head.

"We can't let her do this...Boss!" pleaded Abdul.

"Blame the Emperor," I said.

At that Abdul straighten. He looked at me squarely for several seconds, then nodded okay.

"Set up for Julie to accompany us to see Dr. Billie Kookie."

"Right, Boss," was his glum reply.

Chapter 103

Something about the letters A.E. bothered me. A. E., Anna Elisabeth. A.E.

They'd been on the drawing taken by Willie the Sneak from the Emperor's office, supposedly somewhere in Europe.

Then I realized what had bothered me. A. E. had been missing from my copy of Julie's birth certificate. Why would that be?

I thought about Julie, Anna Elisabeth, and Aunty Dotty living in a select and lavish apartment in downtown San Francisco. Seemingly unsupported.

Surely, even with rent control, no apartment the size of Julie's could be cheap. Was Aunty Dotty's pension enough to possibly cover it?

I decided to snoop a bit into the other end of the Emperor's money trail. Perhaps he was secretly funneling funds to Julie and her family. That is, if he indeed was related, and if, well this was hard to imagine, he was also a family man.

Chapter 104

While Abdul setup our meeting with Dr. Billie Kookie, I took a quiet trip down to City Hall on my lunch hour. I went to the City Records department and checked out a large dusty tome filled with building and housing records.

I wanted to check out who owned Julie's apartment.

In about five minutes of turning flimsy pages, I found out. The owner was one Abdul Dalaah. Abdul!? My moonlighting concierge office-slave?

With a second confirming look, I saw he indeed owned the whole building.

Abdul was definitely a man of more resources than I ever suspected.

And then by accident, I noticed Abdul's name in other places on the page.

I turned several pages forward and back.

Abdul not only owned the apartment house, he owned the whole damn block.

Chapter 105

I was sitting at my desk when Abdul came in. He'd run some errand to get more fax paper. He came in balancing many white rolls in his arms. He looked a little like a modern brown-faced cannibal carrying his bones to work.

"Hey, Boss, I've set up the meeting with Dr. Kookie. Tomorrow at 1:30. We'll be catching him between shows at Moscone."

I nodded. Abdul quickly looked around to see why I hadn't responded more.

I held up a piece of copy paper by the corner, the way a fisherman holds up the tail of dead trout.

"What's that, Boss?" asked Abdul.

"Well, sit down," I said, "Let's talk about it."

"What's it about? The FBI getting after us?"

"Oh no, it's about you. It seems I don't know you that well," I said.

"Oh, shucks, Boss, you know me. We've been working together so long. I'm you're office helper, and moonlighting concierge."

I didn't nod or accept this shuffle.

"Abdul, I have a paper here," I said handing it over the desk. "It says you own Julie's apartment."

Abdul's forehead wrinkled with concern and his mouth nearly disappeared.

"In fact, when I checked the records, it says you own the whole city block, all the apartment houses on it. Abdul, this makes you a moderately rich man."

"Mistake, Boss," said Abdul flustered. "It's is another Abdul Dallah."

"Right," I said.

There was a silence as we both eyed each other. Abdul finally nodded that indeed I wasn't going to buy any bullshit.

"So, little buddy," I said, "You got money in a big way. Explain that to me. You're not who you portray yourself as, the office-slave, moonlight concierge."

"Boss!" protested Abdul.

"Let's hear it, or you're outa here. If I don't know who you are, I don't know what you're doing. You'll be off this case, and Julie and I will go it alone."

"I have money," admitted Abdul. Abdul looked up at the ceiling as if to find a place to start.

"When Roxanna died," he began, "Remember Roxanne? I swore to be a rich man. Remember? Well, I did, I went to school in computers. I got good. I did consulting. Then consulting in a big way. Boss, I'm consulting with huge companies, big governments. And I'm charging arms and legs. Boss, I'm getting rich. But I'm sick of it. I'm retiring. So I make some investments, I buy the buildings. Julie and her family, they aren't rich, they have little, so I give them a break, I give them practically free room in my building."

"Why do people think you are the concierge in your own apartment house?" I asked.

"Oh, well, that was at first a joke. When I bought the building and moved in, I put up the sign "Abdul Dallah, Concierge Extraordinaire!" as a joke. But people, they started coming to my door asking me to fix their sink, or help with the air conditioning. So I helped them. I liked it. They invite me into their homes. They show me their problems. So, I am the concierge. For years, the people in the building, they think I'm there just for them. And so, I meet them, I find out about them. They are a little like my family. I help them with small fixes." Abdul opened his hand in a pleading gesture. "To them, I'm Abdul, the concierge."

"Extraordinaire," I said.

"How rich are you" I asked after a brief pause.

"Well, those buildings, they are investments, a man my age, he must have his pile hidden to sustain him. They are rental income properties, they bring in one or two million...not so much."

"A year or a month?" I asked.

"A month," admitted Abdul. He shrugged sheepishly.

"It is rental income, Boss. It's what allows me to work for you," pleaded Abdul. Oddly, Abdul seemed concerned that indeed he would be fired. As if Morgan's Eagle-Eye Detective Agency meant something to him.

I suppose it did. I needed him.

"Okay," I said, "So you're a success. I can believe it. It's no surprise the way you turn things around here. You can work for whatever idealistic reasons you've got in that brown skull. That I don't care about. It's just the truth is always a good deal to have around."

"Boss, you would treat me different if you didn't think I was poor. You wouldn't let me do the work."

I nodded. It's hard to have a multi-millionaire emptying your waste basket.

"So, can we forget about my millions, and help Julie? She is my friend, and I'm her ...concierge," said Abdul.

"And my office-slave," I said.

"Yes, Boss, please..."

Man, what a mystery life was. Mother Teresa, Abdul...who were these surprising spirits?

I knew I couldn't get rid of him; after all these years he was practically my brother.

I stood and offered my hand. Abdul shook it with jittery enthusiasm.

But in the back of my head, I realized I had an office slave who thought that making one or two million a month was 'not so much.'

At least I knew my answer if he ever asked for a raise.

Chapter 106

Emperor's Comment:

Whew! Close call for Abdul.

Funny how people discriminate against those who know how to make a buck. Put you on some kind of pedestal or monsterize you. When you're just a person who's got pockets sewn in your jeans like everyone else. It's just your pockets hold a bail of money.

Long ago, I discovered why people hide their money. It's because money buys many things. And one of the things it buys is violence.

On a highly idealistic note, for someone denoted by most as a criminal mastermind, of super-excessive wealth, I have a certain philosophical outlook on money. Property, rather. Owning things comes down to the ability to defend it. If you purchase things, you establish a basic right to the defense of your property through the sanctioned violence, represented by police, armies, killing in self-defense, lawyers (now there's a group that does real violence to reality) and such, embedded in the societal structure. This is seen as a legitimate use of violence. But having property means you are willing to exert violence against those who would take it: those who have violence, but no property. Property is a mild form of violence. If you buy a home or car, you are just saying that the established code of violence is on your side, and so you can keep it. People most in touch with this stock handguns under their pillow, which usually only get fired by kids at other kids.

Then the violence buys vast properties of regret.

So why do people see the Emperor as such a violent guy?

I have humongous mountains of cash! See? I have ten-story mountains of would-be violence stacked up! It's just waiting to avalanche down on you...

In truth, however, real violence comes from the nature of the human soul. Property, your ownership rights, the things you slave for, you can hide, limit, or deny. But that black snarl we use to keep our little bowl of doggy chow from other buddy dogs, that's in our hearts.

In reality, I think we need it. I do.

Me, I just say, "Here's five bucks, go see a movie while I eat!"

Or, in the worst case, I let the grasping violence of others be reflected back up themselves. I tip the police about a rival's heist. I call the FBI that a white-slave trader has another 14-year-old runaway in his trunk. I push the buttons of built-in violence.

Why?

Because I am the Emperor, Criminal Mastermind and Controller of All Criminal Destiny! It says so in my job description. I got bucks enough to buy your violent little soul, should I want another. Yeah. I could put your soul on a string and use it as a yoyo. Yeah!

Ha, ha. Grandiosity can be fun.

Here endth the sermon for the day, the plate will be coming by in a minute. Your fellow church goers will lay on violent attitudes unless you lay in a big wad.

Get with it!

Chapter 107

If we were going to be carting Julie through our investigation, I figured we'd better have a bit more protection for her. We'd had heavy gunfire, and attempted kidnappings, all close on my heels as I snooped. If we were to suddenly take a step backwards, I didn't want to bump Julie into the line of fire and have her catch one in the behind.

I dialed a number to the best housekeeper I knew.

"Hello?" was the answer. It was Sugar Ray Mohamed Ali's deep voice, a bit like a bullfrog in a barrel.

"Sugar Ray, it's Morgan," I said.

"Yeah?"

"I've got a job for you, I want you to do some bodyguard work for me," I said.

"Going to be shooting?" asked Sugar Ray.

"I don't know," I said, "But I've got a young client, and she needs some babysitting as we have a meeting or two. I'd pay you to come and watch her back."

"That'll be two hundred bucks an hour," said Sugar Ray.

Man, he was making more than I was! However, he was the biggest walking wall I could think of to put behind Julie.

"Sure," I said. I knew Abdul was good for it. I guess he shouldn't have told me he was a millionaire.

"Be at my office tomorrow, 1:00. Okay?"

"Be there," said the Frankensteinian voice, and he hung up.

Chapter 108

The next day at 12:00 I drove over to pick up Julie. She was dressed like a red fire truck on the way to an emergency. She had on a double-breasted red jacket, ruby silk blouse, and a clingy red sweater-skirt that looked like an embarrassed anaconda had choked her half down. Her feet sported ankle-high red suede boots.

"Is that a disguise?" I skeptically, "We're going to meet a preacher."

"What? You think this red getup says Ph.D. all over it?" said Julie sarcastically.

"No, more like 'Hey, I'm shark bait, you naughty little sexual predators'," I said.

"Precisely. We're meeting a TV evangelist aren't we?" smiled Julie with overt irony.

Well, she had me there.

As we pulled up to my office building a big hulking figure just turned the corner out of sight, walking away. I thought for a minute it was Sugar Ray Mohamed Ali, but he should have been entering my building.

Julie and I walked up the stairs.

Abdul opened the door to meet us.

"Well good! We're all here! Let's be going. We don't want to be missing a single sacred word of the Kookie himself. We also have a narrow window for interviewing in his religiously scheduled day."

I looked at my watch: 1:15. Sugar Ray should have been here by now. We were running a bit late.

"Did anyone call?" I asked.

"No," replied Abdul.

No bodyguard. Damn.

I went over to my little broom closet, opened the door, and fumbled for the vests.

I threw down three of them on the desk.

"Put these on, if you can. Sorry the color isn't red, Julie," I said.

"What are those?" Julie asked. She stood there looking skeptically at the pile of straps and thick material I'd put on the table.

Abdul was frowning.

"They're flack-jackets, Julie," I said.

"They are for stopping bullets from entering and doing massive damage to our internal organs," said Abdul, perking up.

Abdul and I looked at each other with eyebrows raised hopefully.

Julie shook her head.

"No you don't. You're not scaring me out of going with you." With that she scooped up a vest and exited for the hall where the ladies room was marked.

"Back in a minute," she said cheerily.

"Sorry, it didn't work, Boss," said Abdul glumly.

Julie came back a few minutes later, her beautiful figure transformed into something resembling a red duck hunter.

"It doesn't look good," I said.

"Don't give me any flack about it!" said Julie.

"Right, Boss, she's prepared to take flack," said Abdul with resignation.

Julie and I looked at each other. Then we laughed.

Chapter 109

We parked in a dim underground structure adjacent to the Moscone Center. Abdul led the way to a small side door in the Center, a big concrete monument to industrial shows and commercial circuses. Abdul knocked three times on a steel door painted a dull green.

No response.

Julie and I gave Abdul a questioning look. He simply smiled.

"Open sezza me," he muttered, joshingly waving magician's fingers at the unbudging door.

The door swung open.

In its frame stood a huge-shouldered football player dressed in a black tuxedo, complete with little red bow tie like a propeller.

"Can I help you? This is a restricted entrance, clergy and staff only for the Dr. Kookie meet."

Abdul took out a small slip of paper, the size of a dollar bill, and held it up. It held the single word "PRESS" in large letters which I'm sure he'd printed himself on our office printer.

"Sezza Me Daily Journal," said Abdul resolutely.

The football player lowered his huge shoulders and stepped back.

With a merry surreptitious wink, Abdul gestured to Julie and I to follow as he walked through the doorway past the huge doorman.

Julie stepped off, walking with graceful assurance, with me close behind.

The football player bade us follow him down several long corridors. As we walked, we caught a glimpse of the great main hall, a veritable aircraft hangar draped with Christianity about to take off: gold banners, crosses, and great smokestacks of colored balloons strung together, floating at the end of each aisle, each balloon inked with a cross on one side and a car on the other.

I nodded to Julie, "It must be his 'Make a Prayer, Get a Car' sermon tonight."

Julie grimaced, thinking I was joking. I wasn't. I'd read in Abdul's backgrounder that his 'Make a Prayer, Get a Car' sermon was one of the biggest, most lucrative shows for the preacher Kookie. Evidently local car dealers handed out promotional tickets by the scores.

Chapter 110

Our little party halted beside a crimson door. As the tuxedoed football player cautiously knocked, we could hear bellowing, high wails, and low grunting on the other side.

The commotion stopped and the door slid open.

There stood Dr. Kookie himself. He was dressed in long satin-pink robe with a rainbow, a bit like a racing stripe, across his chest. He was tall, with raving grey hair flying out all over his head in a cloud. His eyes were beady blue, a bit glassy like some animal caught in the headlights. His face was tan, puffy, and wrinkled, making him look a bit like a seasoned actor playing someone years older than himself.

"Yes, Brother Elmoe? You're interrupting my speaking in tongues workout," said elderly man. Abruptly taken by some invisible force, the pink-robed preacher raised both hands and shouted.

"Em Hallamakum, Hallepeno Papah!"

"It's the Press, sir," whispered tuxedoed Brother Elmoe.

Dr. Kookie smiled. He looked at Abdul, me, then Julie. He smiled larger on seeing Julie.

"Yes, yes, come in," said Dr. Kookie. "You'll have to excuse my little outburst. When the holy ghost comes down and touches you, you have to raise your voice and speak. You just never know what's going to come out." Then as a smiling aside to us, "It even surprises me sometimes."

"Charming!" said Julie with convincing sincerity.

Julie caught my skeptically raised eyebrow.

"This way," said the preacher, "I have just a short time for an interview. Big prayer meeting tonight, as you undoubtedly know."

The tuxedoed doorman left.

As the three of us followed Dr. Kookie into his dressing room, Julie turned and sassily stuck out her tongue at me.

Dr. Kookie seated himself and waved a hand at three canvass director's chairs that circled around him. After we were seated, Dr. Kookie looked at us a moment in silence, then smiled.

"What paper were you with?" asked Kookie.

"The SezzaMe Daily Journal," replied Abdul, "My name is Abdul Dallah."

"God's slave, yes," said Kookie with a nod. He looked at Julie.

"I'm Julie Veingold," Julie piped up.

"And I'm Morgan Hercules," I said.

Kookie had nodded with each name.

"You seem an unlikely little group for reporters," said the preacher. He folded his hands comfortably across his midriff.

It was obvious he didn't buy it.

"Especially, you Julie, wearing a flack jacket underneath that red blouse."

Julie's face was a traffic light that suddenly turned red.

The preacher smiled and nodded again, "You see I sometimes wear one as well. It's part of show business. Being visible. If you become visible someone will rise out of the crowd of the invisible and hate you for it."

Chapter III

"Dr. Kookie, we're sorry to meet you under false pretenses," I said, "I'm a private investigator. I'm working to help Ms Veingold here."

"Dr. Julie Veingold," injected Julie, "I've a doctorate in pyschological archaeology. We're looking for some information, to help someone who is sick: my....mother."

Julie stole a quick glance at me, but didn't meet my eye.

"Well, if you promise not to talk psycho-babble to me, I promise not to talk theo-babble to you," said the elderly preacher with a gleam in his eye.

"Abdul there is my assistant," I said.

"And I'm Dr. Billie Kookie. Doctorate in Theology from Harvard, Julie. Nice to meet us all, eh?" said Kookie. He sat back with his hands calmly held against his chest.

"So, what can I do for you? Ask your questions," he said. "I'm a little pressed for time. We have a big night tonight with my 'Make a Prayer, Get a Car' sermon."

"What's this about getting cars, if I may ask," said Julie.

"Oh," laughed the preacher, "It's a sermon I give, a well paying one, mind you. You see as a big time preacher, I'm rather heavily involved in raising funds for my ministry. Almost constantly by the way. I admit that sounds crass, but it's part of building a ministry to a highly TV'ified audience these days. You see at base, I've had to accept that I'm an entertainer. Entertaining for God's masses. But hopefully bringing a little light and relief here and there, too."

"And the car sermon?" hinted Julie.

"Yes, well it all came about when I was making a sermon one night in Detroit," laughed Dr. Kookie, "When out of the blue I shouted to my audience 'If you drive a Ford, God wants you to drive a Cadilac!' Well there you are!"

The preacher in pink open his hands to us in a gesture of false modesty. Then he laughed good-naturedly.

"Well, by the end of the week I received a $5,000 donation from the local Cadilac dealers. Sales had gone through the roof. One even contacted me to see if I'd specifically mention the Seville. So my staff and I recognized a good thing when we saw one. Now before we hit town, we make sure to contact the local car dealers to let them know about my up-coming car sermon. We ask that they donate a portion of their increased profits. Most recognize the benefit of my congregation hearing 'the Lord drives a Lexus' pretty quickly."

Preacher Kookie shook his head. "Incredible, huh?"

"And those who don't?" asked Julie.

Kookie laughed. "Well, my staff just mentions that sometimes I've been known to say things like 'the Devil drives a Dodge'. The ministry, of course, sells our stocks in such a car company the morning before the sermon, in case the Press picks it up. But the dealers usually get the hint."

"Don't you think that's kind of a scam?" asked Julie.

"Well, yes it is, Julie. You see I accept that I must make money. My 'Make a Prayer, Get a Car' sermons are decent ways of indirectly making money off my parishioners. It has funded my new Lord's Hospital, and the Kookie Children's Cancer Ward. And they get a car!" laughed Kookie. "But don't think too badly of me really. It's just good Christian capitalism. You have to go with what your society hands you. At least I don't employ a couple million underage adolescents selling 50 cents worth of cookies for 3 bucks a pop, like those Girl Scouts. Now there's an organization that likes to rip off minors!"

Julie's face was passive, unimpressed.

"Please, don't think me too brazen," chuckled Preacher Kookie, "My mission is not totally making money. You see, I help those masses in front of me, out of touch with their God, and out of touch with themselves, to get in touch. I'm an entertainer, but I also bring God back into view for the hungering many. You see when my audience attends my show, and I have them testify, they see real tears of misery, real tears of joy, real tears of desire for the sublime. Once again, they feel God is among them. Who would you or I be to tell them God is not among them? Shared there among them. Julie, I tell you honestly, my congregation is Godly to me."

"Do you even believe in God?" asked Julie.

Dr. Billie Kookie smiled. It appeared he felt it unnecessary to answer, but for this young woman in red he would bend.

"You know, for someone with a doctorate in Theology, it's a surprisingly hard question to answer. It would probably be a good thesis in psychological archeology to determine when and if the church lost its belief in God, and started believing in its congregation. I've never seen God, Julie. Not once when I do my priestly jig for cash. But the people I see before me, they see God, and like a blind man before the sighted, I have to take their word for it. I wouldn't tell them otherwise."

Chapter 112

"But enough about me. You seem to be a little band on a quest," said Kookie pointing two angelic fingers our way. "And being 75% holy man and 25% laughing trickster, it's my job to help you with your quest."

"Dr. Kookie," I began, "Have you ever heard of the Emperor?"

"Yes, in a certain branch of Judaic studies, the Kabala, there is a codification of the Tree of Life embodied in the Tarot deck. The Emperor is a card of the Major Arcana. It represents the ruler of all, which represents how we see the world. It is also called The Window, through which we see and by which we are seen. It pertains to our vision. A very powerful card. The Emperor is the guardian of your Kingdom, judging and ruling on all that enters or goes out. If your heart is mean and penurious, your Emperor, the guardian of the gate, will make sure you live in poverty. If your heart is grand and abundant," Kookie flashed his eyebrows up and down in a Groucho-Marx signal meaning 'like me', "your Emperor will permit you to live in grand abundance."

"No, we are looking for a criminal master mind, known as the Emperor, a real person. We believe he is related to Julie, and we desperately need to contact him," I said.

"I don't believe I've had any dealings with such a person, I'm sorry," said Kookie.

"We believe you may have received some funds from him or his organization around 1987. Do you recall any unusual donations about that time?" I asked.

"Well, 1987 was the year I founded Yahweh World. Our Christian amusement park specially designed for the Christian family. You know the Yahweh World motto: Enjoy a little bit of heaven here on earth? A place where Christian families can retreat and unburden from the cares of the world. Even for just a little while."

Julie's eyes went to the ceiling, and then she asked, "And how did you get the inspiration to build Yahweh World? Watching the Disney Channel?"

Kookie laughed heartily, "No, Julie, it was actually while I was reading the Disney World Annual Report. You have to be astute and learn if you're in the entertainment business."

Kookie turned back to me. "That year I indeed received an incredible anonymous donation. Nearly $250 million dollars. It was enough to fund Yahweh World with one check! I didn't take a dollar from my congregation to fund it. Oddly, that same year someone reported us to the IRS. So there we were with all that money, the IRS looking at us, and we had to build Yahweh World."

"You've never met the Emperor? Would you like to contact him?" asked Abdul.

"Well, yes, if it was his money, to thank him for the new west wing of the Heavenly Hotel."

"You see we do give a little bit back to the people, Julie. I can see you don't believe it. But me, I'm afraid I count myself as one of the believers. You'll have to come to see Yahweh World someday. It's harmless recreation. A beautiful place. A place devoted to fun and clean spirits. No harm in that. My new project is to build an International Airport for the Handicapped."

"Funded by the Emperor?" said Abdul.

"Well, if that's so, then bless his soul," said Kookie with his eternal smile.

"Well, thank you for your time, Dr. Kookie," I said rising from my chair.

"No problem, I wish you well, pilgrims, on your quest."

"Thank you," I said.

Julie got up from his chair, her face clouded.

"Julie, I hope you find the answer for your mother," said Kookie sincerely.

Julie nodded thanks.

Kookie opened his hands and closed them. "You know, I can see you're convinced I'm only in it for the money. But it's not so. I do good works, too. There are those that really need me. My old Daddy, he was in show business, too. And he taught me to always give them their money's worth. Let them hear what they need to hear, a song, a prayer, whatever is on their minds and hearts. Sometimes they need to hear the voice of God."

Intrigued, Abdul turned and asked, "What did your father do in show business?"

Kookie grinned, "Back in Vaudeville, he was a ventriloquist."

And then Abdul began to laugh. He grabbed his ribs and really began to ha ha.

Then Kookie caught it and was soon laughing so hard that tears were forming in his eyes. Shaking their heads and showing their teeth like dogs chewing bones, they were staggering, gasping, speechless with mirth. For one moment, they had their arms on each other's shoulders holding themselves up, weak with laughter.

"A ventriloquist!" gasped Kookie bleary-eyed. Abdul howled.

Julie and I looked at this pair yukking for all they were worth.

Then we helped Abdul from the room still hiccoughing with laughter.

Chapter 113

After Abdul recovered enough to drive, he fit the key into the ignition, saying, "That Kookie, he's a funny guy."

Julie grimaced, "Seems all he's interested in is money."

"No, Julie," corrected Abdul, "It isn't making scads of money that's good or bad. It's what you do with it after you get it that counts."

Chapter 114

Emperor's Comment:

That Kookie: what a card! Money and priestly works, sounds like a fun combination. I'll have to contribute to that International Airport for the Handicapped! What's the harm in relieving the pain of the deluded masses, when it's up to the individual to save himself from the Emperor?

Chapter 115

"So what did we learn from Dr. Kookie?" asked Julie, as she threw down the useless flack jacket on my desk, returning from down the hall.

"We learned we need to see the next person on our list, Dr. Needler," I said.

Abdul nodded. "I'll get to work on it right away, Boss."

Chapter 116

Just so you don't go putting me on a pedestal, I, Morgan Hercules, have committed a crime.

It was when I was twenty or so. Young. I was walking with my then girlfriend KJ Switzerman around the little lake at the Frank Lloyd Wright Civic Center in Marin. We were taking an afternoon walk around the cattail-lined banks, walking shoulder to shoulder, when a black kid, maybe fourteen, came into sight. He was standing stock still. He was still the way a setter or cat is when watching something important or threatening.

In front of him stood five white kids, about the same age. They were standing in a ragged group looking at him. They were absolutely silent. One of the white kids was smaller, with long lanky blond hair, his head barely reaching the shoulder of his friends. As KJ and I walked by this silent little group, I noticed the smaller kid holding an open pocket knife with about a four-inch blade down against his thigh.

The expressions on the kids' faces were blank as they stood looking at this black kid.

KJ and I walked by.

I didn't register that something intense was going on until I'd walked KJ around the bend. Then I realized it.

I didn't go back.

I realize now I was mistaken. I should have gone back and thrown that little white kid with his knife in the lake. I had the power to throw the whole bunch of them in the damn lake. But at that point, I didn't know anything about the Wrath of God. I was afraid to interfere in the stalemate. I didn't realize all this and help a lone black adolescent who was standing still for his life.

So, that's my crime.

I convicted myself.

Chapter 117

Emperor's comment:

So Morgan convicts himself of sins of omission. Ha, what would he think of me and my grand sins of commission? What would he think if he unknowingly turned the children of entire nations into beggars....by omission or commission? Welcome brother convict! A single black kid or a nation's children in poverty! Shoulder that guilt! We deserve it. Every great criminal sitting in the electric chair knows he threw the switch on himself.

And that blue electric light zapping down through your skull, scrambling your Soul and Self: it is the Wrath of God!

Chapter 118

That evening I called Sugar Ray Mohamed Ali to find out what happen.

"Hello?"

"Sugar Ray, where were you? You were supposed to come with me to bodyguard at 1:00. What happened?"

There was a long pause on the line.

"I was there, but your clerk, Abdul told me to go home."

What? Well, Abdul hadn't known about Sugar Ray. But why wouldn't he just have him stay to find out?

"Well, can you come in tomorrow?" I said, "We still need you."

"Can't got a job," said Sugar Ray.

"Look! I need you!"

"Can't."

I took a deep breath.

"Okay, okay, another time," I said. I decided to hang up.

"Morgan?"

"Yeah?"

"Watch your back," said Sugar Ray.

"What? What do you mean by that?" I asked.

The phone went dead.

Abdul came into the office. He seemed more cheerful than normal, he was actually whistling a bit through his front teeth, a small canary like song.

"Abdul?" I said.

"Yes, Boss, I'm getting on the Dr. Needler meeting."

"Did somebody come by to be Julie's bodyguard yesterday?"

Abdul hesitated one second, dropping his whistle like a teapot taken off the stove.

"Yeah, Boss. A big monster black guy. He wanted to see you about being a bodyguard. I said no, we don't need one, and sent him on his way. Did I do wrong?"

"Yes, I'd asked him to come. Why didn't you say so when Julie and I arrived?"

"Sorry, it is slipping my mind, I guess."

"Slipping your mind like the millions of bucks people send you each month?"

Abdul made a sheepish duck.

"Aw, Boss, you're not going to keep throwing that at me, like some couple getting a divorce, are you? I'm making a mistake is all. I will hire bodyguards for all of us if you want me."

"No," I said. "Let's just get on with meeting Dr. Needler."

I let the subject drop. But that distant bell of truth, that told me who I was, where I was, and what I was doing, it sure wasn't ringing.

Not even a little ding.

Chapter 119

"There it is," said Abdul, nodding his head over the steering wheel at a big marble entryway to what looked like a city mausoleum. It was actually the R&D branch of a pharmaceutical company. Chiseled into the shiny pink marble in deep Romanesque characters were the words: Needler, Cutter, and Saw Pharmaceuticals.

"Dr. Needler works in the new wonder drug department, even though he now owns the company," said Abdul.

"I hope they don't have bodies laid out on tables," said Julie with a shiver.

"Only little furry ones, I'm sure," replied Abdul.

I got out of the car and held the door open for Julie.

"You needn't do that," said Julie, affixing her monocle as if screwing a pop bottle into her eye. "I've opened car doors myself for years. Vestiges of gallantry are not necessary these days."

"Sometimes I look into my clean laundry and vestiges is all I have to wear," I said.

"Clearly," said Julie.

The three of us walked up the stone steps. A small security chamber, built like a theater box office, complete with a guard inside, asked us our names through thick glass. I stated our business and that we had an 11:00 o'clock visit with Dr. Needler. The guard looked down and checked his clipboard. We must have been on the list. With three high beeps, a glass door slowly swung open, and Julie, Abdul, and I entered the glass entry way.

The building lobby was covered with many potted plants, palms, and vines covering the floor, polished tables, and hanging from walls like extra thick cobwebs. The place had a distinct jungle atmosphere, and the scent of soil, fungus, and...something else...damp stumps.

A small, bald man in a suit approached with an unctuous smile.

"Welcome to Needler, Cutter, and Saw. You're here to see Dr. Needler?"

I nodded yes.

"Right this way. I see you're admiring our many plants. Each one is a South American import. And a beauty to us. Several have been the sources of new drugs that earned us millions. So we keep a lobby full of our prizes."

Julie nodded, "Very impressive."

"One of them actually eats worms," said the bald man over his shoulder as he walked off, leading the way.

"I did that when I was only three," I said straight faced to Julie.

"Then you went out and killed yourself a Bar, I'm sure," muttered Julie.

I smiled.

"No actually I ran for a drink of water."

Chapter 120

After walking down several corridors, moving from thick plush green rug to white tiled linoleum, through a heavy traffic of white-coated workers wheeling carts covered mysteriously with blankets, the little bald man stopped in front of a black door. I looked and the door was not painted, it was varnished black ebony.

The small man knocked on the door. He then pushed a button on a small intercom box built into the wall.

"Dr. Needler, your 11:00 appointment is here," he said leaning into the box as if he enjoyed talking to a wall.

"Send them in, please," squawked the box.

I heard a buzz and a heavy mechanical click. The black door slowly swung inward. It was as if we were being invited into a vault where valuables were kept.

The small bald man raised an inviting palm toward the door.

"Thanks," I said and stepped into Needler's office.

When I first glanced around I thought the walls were entirely covered with glass aquariums. But on second look, the fish inside were knives of all sorts, shapes, and colors, many with exotic twisted blades. They were just hanging like fish mounted in the glass cases.

A man in a smock was standing up behind a black desk, his hands down on the desktop for balance. He was an older man, with wizened face, heavy black eyebrows, and pinched mouth. His smile, showing canines, was a cross between something you might see on a Doberman pincher and an elderly man stuck by surprise with a pin.

"I am Dr. Needler. Please sit down," he said.

Julie was inspecting the many cases of knives around the walls as she walked forward.

"You like my little collection?" asked Needler to Julie.

"Well, it is exotic," said Julie noncommittally.

"These are all ancient sacrificial knives. Beautiful as they are, each one has killed at least one human. Some of them hundreds," said Needler, with a grandiose gesture of a king sweeping his arms to indicate his realm.

"Do you have a Jeffrey Dalhmer section?" I asked.

"You jest. But, I actually do own a scalpel from the alleged Jack the Ripper...an interesting little piece. Very hard to come by, personally."

"Especially for those who personally came by it," I said.

"And you are?" asked the smocked physician.

"My name is Morgan Hercules. This is Julie Veingold, my client. And that is my assistant, Abdul Dallah."

"Very good," nodded Needler.

Abdul had held to the back of the room, when suddenly he pointed at a small ancient drill of some sort.

"What is this, Doctor?" Abdul asked pointing at the drill.

"Oh that. It doesn't really fit my collection, I know. It's a drill used by the Medieval Mendicis. They used it to drill a hole in a patient's head to let out evil spirits. It, of course, killed more people than it saved."

Looking uncomfortable surrounded by these gruesome tools, Julie asked, "Why doesn't it fit your collection here?"

"Oh, well, it was meant to save lives," shrugged Needler.

Chapter 121

The doctor sat down at his desk and folded his hands, "Shall we get started? I understand you have questions for me? An investigation?"

Julie was not to be put off right away, "Doctor, why do you collect such deadly artifacts?"

"Oh, physicians, you know how they are. Something about them is interested in such things. The horror and ghastly parts of life. I mean you have to if you want to constantly deal with the sick. Unless you're into it just for the money. You know, of course, the guillotine was invented by a French physician?"

I nodded yes.

"It started a whole 19th century trend in operations! It was no longer necessary to save the patient. Merely cut out the offending part."

"Of course, the prospects of recovery were mighty small," said Abdul.

"Right," chuckled the Doctor, "But the operation was always a success. A medical joke, there." Needler smiled his pin-stuck smile at Julie.

I saw Julie try to stifle a cringe.

Chapter 122

"Doctor Needler, we're conducting an investigation, trying to locate a donor for Julie's...." I hesitated, glancing at Julie, "Mother, who has Leukemia."

"Is she in a bad way?" asked the doctor to Julie.

Julie nodded.

"I actually know very little about Leukemia," said the doctor, "For me, if you can't drug it, cut it out, or ignore it, then there's nothing you can do about it. It's of no medical interest."

"No, we weren't exactly looking for medical advice," I said.

"Well, we are working on a secret drug, very close to the market, one that rejuvenates the human organ systems. But we don't do experimentation on humans here. I'm sorry. We merely shake and bake little animals...another medical joke there!" said Needler as an aside.

"We're actually hoping that you'd help us locate someone. The donor we're looking for. Perhaps you could provide us information."

"Who is this person that you want information about?"

"Julie's grandfather...he has a certain criminal reputation. He is known as the Emperor.

"Sorry, I don't know who that is," said Needler. He gave Julie a sympathetic nod like a doctor forced to operate without the drugs.

"We have information that you may have received funds from the Emperor, perhaps in a donation, sometime around 1987?"

"How would you know that?" said Needler, his face closing with concern.

"An FBI report," said Abdul coolly.

I nodded in confirmation.

Needler sat silently for a minute.

"Have we got FBI informants here?" asked Needler. "Because if they're in here messing around with our experiments in a free capitalist state where you can make money selling drugs...I'll...I'll...go to the President! I will. I've sent him a couple of good pills or two to try out. I know how to get his attention."

"No, Doctor," I said, "We intercepted the report in a, shall we say, extra curricular way..."

"Meaning?"

"Meaning there was no indication that the government was fiddling in your works."

"Okay, good," said Needler, somewhat relieved. He sat back in his chair.

"Did you receive a large donation of funds around 1987?" I asked.

"Well, frankly, I did. I was still researching my wonder drug. Begging for funds. I had to support myself with a private practice. Doing quickie operations. I was doing about three hysterectomies a day, when this grant came through. It was huge. It enabled me to stop operating, write a proposal, and buy my way into this company. I brought in my drug, and it began to work. We're still years from getting an FDA release, but this company has pinned its future on it."

"Who gave you the money?"

"The Emporium of Empathic Medicine, or some such name."

I looked at Julie and nodded.

"You don't know anything else about this grant, or the Emperor?"

"Nope, I took the money and ran."

Just then a little buzzer went off behind the doctor. The old man straightened and then smiled at us.

"Excuse me, that signals time for my next inoculation." Needler began working his sleeve up his arm. He then opened a drawer and pulled out a small bottle of pink solution, and a hypodermic needle that Frankenstein would have been afraid of.

"This is the latest version of my new wonder drug," said the doctor. "I am the only human to ever experience it. It is a serum that prevents disease by energizing the immune system. In laymen's terms it makes your body real mean to germs."

Abdul, Julie and I watched in silence as Needler drew the solution up into the needle, then shot himself in the arm.

"It's a new drug, and kind of hard on the body," said Needler. He closed his eyes. When he opened them again, he gave us a dreamy smile.

"Of course, I take a bit of the edge off with cocaine."

"Thank you, Doctor Needler, I guess that will be all." I said rising from my chair.

"Sorry I can't offer you any of this," said Needler patting his little pink bottle. "It's not ready for the public yet. But at least there's one wonder drug available to you that cures all!"

"What drug is that?" said Julie

"Money!" Needler laughed. It was another medical joke.

"So much for health care..." muttered Julie.

Chapter 123

As we rode back to Julie's apartment, Julie said, "I wonder why the Emperor would give money to Dr. Needler? What does a criminal mastermind get out of that?"

"Perhaps he sees it as a way of developing new drugs?" said Abdul.

"Well, it seems the money definitely cut down on the rate of useless hysterectomies..." I said.

"Think of that old man, locked in that vault, with all those death instruments, putting drugs in his arm," sighed Julie, puzzled.

I looked at Abdul and Abdul looked at me.

"Seems to have taken a lot of dangerous things off the street," Abdul said.

"Perhaps the Emperor was eliminating the competition?" I said.

"Naw," said Julie with a dismissive shrug.

Chapter 124

Julie, Abdul, and I agreed to meet the next day to go see the last man on our list, Charles Ashe.

"We'll pick you up at the apartment around noon," said Abdul.

"We don't seem to be making much progress," said Julie. "Is this always the way your cases go?" Julie gave me a skeptical look.

"Yes, but one usually finds what one looks for," I said, "If you look long enough."

"And know what you're looking for," said Abdul.

"Which we don't," said Julie.

"Finding out what you're looking for, that's the adventure," I said. "You should know that, you're trained in psychological archeology, right?"

"Morgan, you give me shit about my degrees, and I'll be looking for a hammer for a cranial implant," rebuffed Julie.

I smiled and put on my hat.

"Less bickering among friends," said Abdul to the car mirror.

"Look, Julie, we'll find him. Believe a little in us...please," I said, "Because...after all these years as a detective, I know this: you also find what you believe in."

Chapter 125

Emperor's Comment:

Right on, Morgan. And the minute you start believing, you're on your way to making it come true. At one crystal moment in my youth, I wanted a zillion dollars. That's what I believed was right for me. Well, folks here I am. There's my zillion dollars right over there in that huge pile of bank books on my bed. The next step, is then going beyond what you believe.

Chapter 126

"Boss, look at this," said Abdul, putting a hastily jotted piece of paper in front of me, "I just got this off the police scanner."

I knew that Abdul would occasionally sit with headphones on doing his work. To clients it looked like my assistant was happily listening to his Walkman as he typed. In actuality, I'd discovered Abdul was tuned into the police short-wave band, monitoring the busy city's police calls. What was unnerving about it was that occasionally Abdul would burst out laughing for no apparent reason.

I read the note:

CAR 54 RESPONDING: WE HAVE A RAVING NUT, NAKED AS A JAY BIRD, DISORIENTED POLK AND VAN NESS. CLAIMS TO BE PRIEST DR. BILLIE KOOKIE. CONFIRM?

CAR 54 DR. KOOKIE HAS BEEN REPORTED MISSING. YOU MAY HAVE THE MAN. CONFIRM.

CAR 54: MAN CLAIMING TO BE KOOKIE ALSO CLAIMS TO HAVE BEEN KIDNAPPED, DRUGGED. GIVEN A TRUTH SERMON, HIS WORDS. MAN INDEED APPEARS DRUGGED. WAS WANDERING STREET NAKED, RAVING. REFUSES TO TALK, RESISTING. GIVING ONLY NAME, RANK, AND SWISS BANK ACCOUNT NUMBER.

CONFIRMED. IT'S HIM. KEEP QUIET. FRIEND OF MAYOR. OUT.

ACKNOWLEDGED. AND GET THIS, HE SAYS GOD DRIVES AN UNMARKED CAR.

I looked up at Abdul. "You know, I think we have a problem, there," I said pointing at my office phone.

Abdul nodded.

"Want me to do something, Boss?" asked Abdul.

I shook my head. "Not for now."

Chapter 127

We picked up Julie at her apartment, Abdul driving his beat up old Mercedes Benz. It was roomy and comfy with big seats of plum-color leather. Julie had been waiting on the front steps of the apartment. She was dressed entirely in black in a long-sleeve dress with high elevated shoulders. As she walked toward us, the dress was long enough that it swished like a fish tail at her ankles. She dropped into the back seat with a jounce.

"Welcome, Julie," called Abdul at the wheel.

I nodded approvingly at Julie's clothes. "Nice," I said.

"So today we go to see Charles Ashe," said Julie, ignoring me.

"What do we know about him?" I said to Abdul.

"Very little, he's an obscure person," replied Abdul.

"I've read a bit about him in my research," said Julie.

"Pray tell, tell," I said.

"Well, he was basically a well-known critic. Actually a much hated one, known for slamming other's philosophical works. He could tear apart a thesis with such skill no scholar wanted him to even read a paper. He had high pretensions on a philosophical level, even proclaiming himself the next Heidegger, which would be seen once his masterpiece was published. A treatise or some such on the nature of nature."

"It has implications for natural law, the correct order of things, which some would believe we humans should follow," interrupted Abdul, throwing this information back over his shoulder.

Julie raised an approving eyebrow at Abdul and nodded this was true.

"Abdul, you always surprise me that you're so well read," said Julie.

Abdul nodded, the smallest of appreciative bows he could muster in the confinement of the car.

"He's the brains, I's just the muscle," I said.

"No kidding," said Julie flatly.

"So, did Ashe publish his masterpiece?" I asked.

"No, he really pretty much disappeared from sight years ago. He stopped writing criticism. Mainly to work on his chef d'oeuvre, but it's never seen the light of day. The scholarly world breathed a sigh of relief, I'm sure."

We had crossed town out into the peninsula and woven our way over Devil's Slide and into the San Mateo hills. After a half-hour of driving, Abdul reached a wooded area on the coast highway, and then turned onto an unmarked gravel road. Bouncing and bumping, we traveled several miles back into a canyon, tree limbs and the canyon walls getting closer overhead as we went in, dimming our passage. Finally, we came to a big gate, made of cyclone fencing, that was tall enough to keep King Kong out. The gate was covered with signs, many in neon orange lettering that said, Keep Out, No Hunting, No Loitering, No Visitors, No Soliciting, Trespassers Will Be Shot, and even one that said Trespassers Will Be Violated. A thorough job. A small wooden box with a yellow button hung on a timber by the gate.

Abdul and I went out and stood by the box with the yellow button.

"What did you tell him about us when you set up the meeting?" I asked.

Abdul reached out and pushed the yellow button.

"Nothing," said Abdul.

"He doesn't know we're coming?" I asked.

"Who the hell is out there? Go away, Cretins. No visitors! None! Go away! And don't push that button again!" squawked the box with the button.

Abdul bent toward the box.

"Pool cleaners!" shouted Abdul.

I looked at him. "Why not just cry 'Land Shark'?" I said in dismay, "That has about as much chance of getting us in—"

Just then a big vibration set up in the huge gate, and it slowly began to draw back, a little like a small naval destroyer being first launched into a harbor.

Abdul looked at me and smiled. "He has a pool and pool service," said Abdul, "I checked."

I nodded.

"Let's go introduce ourselves to Mister Ashe."

Chapter 128

We pulled through the gate and then drove for another quarter mile into a deepening ravine. The passage grew darker, the low overhanging forest canopy and bushes crowding in on us like people carrying huge black umbrellas. The road became two tire paths that actually wound around redwood trunks, some thicker than telephone booths, that attempted to block the way.

Finally we pulled up to a large grey stone house. It was three stories high, with a slate grey facade, a few narrow windows, and a large wooden door that instead of door knobs, had two heavy metal rings.

"Everything but the moat," I said.

"And the dragon," said Julie uneasily.

"And the dungeon," concurred Abdul.

The three of us got out of the car and walked warily up the stone steps to the wooden door.

I knocked and my knuckles produced practically no sound on the heavy timbers.

The door swung open, and there stood an intensely angry little man. He was round bodied, shiny bald, with fiercely black eyebrows that were flapping with his anger like bat wings.

"Who the hell are you! Get off my property! What's this pool man bullshit? Take off!"

"We've come to talk with Charles Ashe," I said. I noticed the man was wearing a black waist coat, and oddly black tights with mirrored-sequined slippers.

"Excuse me, Morgan, but this is Mr. Ashe," Julie interrupted me, smiling sweetly. She turned smiling upon the small belligerent troll before us.

"I've read your work, Mr. Ashe, I'd like to know more," said Julie, and she walked into the black castle, passed the angry troll, leaving Abdul, the little bald man, and I standing looking bewildered.

We all shrugged and followed her into the dark house.

Chapter 129

Julie was standing alone in a big hallway, with the skin of a dead bear, complete with head and grinning fangs, at her feet. She'd stopped to wait for us, not knowing where to go.

Charles Ashe looked at Julie, standing in her high-shouldered black dress as if awaiting mourners at a funeral.

He sniffed, "My mother used to have a dress like that. Except it had burned holes in it all over the chest." Ashe looked over at me, "She was a chain smoker...killed her at 27..."

"We'd like to speak to you, Mr. Ashe," I said.

"This way," said the little bald man gruffly.

He shuffled away in his sequined-slippers to another door down the hallway. Abdul, Julie, and I followed, Julie bending in the doorway to look around before actually entering.

Ashe was now seated at a large highly polished black-cherry desk. There were many papers, books, small trinkets that looked like black glass animals, and even a quill pen on the desktop. Surprisingly large windows lit the background of the room, showing a slaggy landscape, rimmed with deep forest verdure, and a large still pool filled with mirroring black water. What was once a beach umbrella over a patio table, was now the hanging place of tattered rags, like a shipwreck sail or distress signal.

Now seated, Ashe addressed Julie formally.

"So, you've read my work?" he asked, "Someone as pretty and young as you?"

"My name's Dr. Julie Veingold. I have a Ph. D. in psychological archaeology," said Julie.

"Good bogus research, I bet," smiled the bald man.

"You are direct, *Mister* Ashe," said Julie. She emphasized Mister, implying that he was definitely not *Doctor*.

"Degrees are unimportant, it's the thought that counts," sneered Charles.

"Like your Big Stomp theory?" said Julie.

"You've heard about it? I've never published the final work, you can know little if anything about it."

"What is the Big Stomp theory, if a layman may ask?" I asked.

Charles Ashes' hands went to three black leather tomes stacked beside him, which he patted with great care, as if they were living cats or something.

"It's this, my work, which I keep here with me," he said.

Julie turned my way, "The Big Stomp theory is an extension of the Astronomical Big Bang Theory. It is the biological equivalent, am I not right?" said Julie.

Ashe shook his head, "At least you are speaking English, we can use that as a start. Now let's see if I can communicate it a little better to you."

"Julie's joke here is that in the Big Bang Theory, the universe started out with a big bang that sent all the stars and matter flying, just every which way. And we, as animal mistakes, live on the flying debris."

Charles looked at me to see if I was following.

I nodded.

Abdul was walking around the room, lifting objects, as he listened.

"The Big Stomp theory doesn't deal with the laws of stars, however. It deals with the true natural law of animals. Of evolution. How we as animal societies, whether rats in an alley, gangs of crabs scuttling under rocks, or human beings exterminating the neighboring tribes, behave according to the laws of nature."

"It is a mechanistic, fatalistic view, if rumors hold," inserted Julie.

"And if it's true, it's true, mechanistic and fatalistic, not withstanding."

"Well, we're really here to ask you a few questions in another direction," I said.

"No, I'd like to hear about the Big Stomp," said Julie. "As one bogus researcher to the keeper of truth."

I could see Julie found Ashe quite irritating.

"Certainly," said Charles Ashe, bowing his head slightly. I could see Ashe was enjoying his role as enlightener of the ignorant, one he evidently hadn't played in years.

"My research shows that Darwin did not have it right. That the nature of competition didn't forge different species and diversity among animals. No, nature has a bigger plan. We, that is, all animals strive to populate unendingly. We do so in rather creative ways. Compare the jellyfish to the butterfly and see the creative ways creatures have come up with for making a living. And the more creative and successful, the bigger the population."

"However, my theory of the Big Stomp is that nature always follows the equalizing law of flattening populations. Meaning that creativity and success is nothing in the face of natural law."

"Say what?" I said.

"He means that as populations become successful, and expand, nature naturally provides a balancing wave of depopulation," said Julie.

"Well, that clears that up," I said, mystified.

Charles Ashe smiled on me with troll-like good humor, probably because he enjoyed a good dunce.

"Well, sir, it's this way. When animal groups become successful, and grow to a certain size, nature comes along and gets rid of them. For example, a boy turns over a rock at the beach exposing a writhing populace of crabs, a successful little batch of crustaceans. And precisely because there's so many, the boy smashes the rock down on them, squashing all but a wriggling few."

"Ciopinno," I said in mock-wonder.

"Or rats in an alley discover an abundant food source, and succeed in the city. Eventually, because of the population size, disease strikes and kills nearly the entire population, or the city exterminator comes and wipes them out. So it's true with all animal populations."

"I assume that includes Los Angeles?" I said.

"Even more so! Good one there...?" asked Charles, hinting for my name.

"Morgan," I said.

"Yes, Morgan, even for successful human populations. They become creative, adapt, solve the problems of subsistence and shelter, then nature takes over. At a certain point, nature provides the Big Stomp. New diseases, ebola, AIDS, famine, neutron bombs, meaningless wars, these overtake the population and decimate it. That is the natural law."

"And the impact of that theory?" I asked.

"Obvious. Ask any Viet Nam war veteran who discovered that valor, bravery, intelligence, athletic skill all meant nothing toward survival when the napalm bomb dropped next door. Burning bodies, no matter how skilled or creative are still bodies running in flames."

"So human endeavor goes for naught," said Abdul looking now at Charles Ashe.

"Well, yes, my little brown man," said Charles. "When nature provides the big stomp, only the few stragglers on the outer fringes of the population are spared. Not due to any skills or understanding of their own, mind you, only because they were not in the middle of the pile when the rock slammed down."

Ashe patted the three black tomes beside him. "It's all in here."

"Your thesis?" I nodded.

"Why haven't you ever publish it?" asked Julie.

"What's the point?" said Charles Ashe proudly. "Warn the world they're under the poised foot of Mother Nature? No, that would only draw me into the middle of the pile. Stompable, so to speak."

"No, the conclusion of my research is, of course, to separate. To avoid the big stomp, a smart human will separate from the pack and live as detached as possible. As an individual, outside the confines of human service, there the individual has the slightest chance to survive."

"And so you live apart in this castle with your depressing theories," Julie said.

"Yes, and fortunately, I received a large grant once, which allowed me to do just that. Ironically, it was a grant to enable me to complete and publish my research, but of course, ironically, it enabled me to build this house and live separate and at ease. So I don't have to publish. There's no point. At least not until I'm gone..."

"What a pigmy view of existence," said Julie.

"Mother Nature has always enjoyed stomping pigmies as well," laughed Ashe.

Chapter 130

"This grant you received, the one that allowed you not to publish your work, when did you receive it?" I asked.

"Oh, sometime around 1987, when I bought this house and moved from the city. I swore I'd never write a review of scholars' bilious theories again."

"So you came up with some of your own," said Julie. "That you won't publish. I bet those little pet black books are actually empty."

"You know what, Julie, I bet you and I have something in common," replied Ashe.

Julie unblinking, said, "What?"

"One of your beauty, or me of my bald-pated ugliness, don't we just feel the terrible weight of having humans around us every minute?"

Julie looked at Charles Ashe and I could see she understood what he was getting at.

"You see, it's pointless," said Ashe, "You can't serve with them, or save them. So why be flailed by them? Right, Julie? You're not one that lives in the middle of the pile are you? You live way outside on the safe fringe, like me? Right?"

Julie stood blankly without reply, her black dress falling around her like a mourning robe.

"What a knucklehead," Julie said.

Chapter 131

"No, Julie!" replied Ashe getting perturbed. "I'll tell you something: I'm not some unconscious pabulum sucking human following the subliminal beliefs and destiny set out by my mama and papa. Are you, Julie? PH. D. of psychological archeology? Are you the unconscious scion of your mother and father's values? Huh? But me? No, I learned early! See this?"

Ashe pointed abruptly at his shining pate, now turning red with white blotches.

"See those, on my head, the head the makes me so ugly? Those white blotches are scars! You see, I told you my mother was a chain smoker! So I learned as a baby what you could expect from your mother! Hot ashes raining down on your head! Pompeii for a childhood!"

Julie's mouth, and indeed mine, shriveled at Ashe's ghastly hairless dome.

"So see, Julie, Dr. Veingold, I learned what you could expect from family, and saw early, you'd better not take in the world through their smoke-filled eyes. I was happy when she was gone. And I knew I had to look around and take a hard cold look at the world and see it as it was."

"And this is what I see," said Ashe patting the black books piled beside him.

"So now I live separate. I don't take on the projections of that world. I live, a bit like you, in your black dress, a little like a house spider waiting patiently alone in her web. Ready to catch those little flies with your PH. D.? Right, Julie? But you see Julie, at least I know, and maybe you don't. I don't even want the flies."

"A triumph of knowing," sneered Julie.

"You've chosen a convincing system of beliefs, but I don't believe what you've chosen is good for you," interrupted Abdul.

Ashe waved a dismissing hand at my office assistant, "Neither is the Big Stomp, there Mister Untouchable. I bet that's your caste, isn't it?"

"I am a concierge," said Abdul smiling idiotically.

"He's a good and caring person. And at least he's not the little bald doorman of the Big Stomp!" said Julie, indignantly.

Chapter 132

I could see Ashe was visibly stung by Julie's repost.

His shoulder's raised, and he stretched his neck uncomfortably. Then he fixed all three of us with a deep frown.

"This interview is over."

Ashe stood, his chest barely rising above the level of his three precious black tomes.

"That's okay," said Julie, "We're looking for a man, *unlike you*, of immense influence and capabilities, one who actually exerts a rather big albeit black influence on this world. A rich man. We are looking for a man known as *the Emperor...*" said Julie. Julie made way to leave, implying we certainly hadn't found such a person.

Riled, Ashe spoke evenly, "I am the Emperor."

Then he tapped himself theatrically on the chest.

Julie turned back opened-mouthed. Both Abdul and I froze.

Julie stood looking at Ashe glaring back at her with tauntingly raised eyebrows.

Julie stepped forward to the edge of Ashe's desk and slapped him as hard as she could.

Chapter 133

Shaken, Ashe raised his hand to his cheek as if to catch the pain.

"Of course, I was speaking figuratively," said Ashe a bit in shock.

"Julie, he's not the Emperor," Abdul said, "He *received* money from the Emperor."

"Oh," said Julie. I could see she was taken aback by her mistake.

"I took him literally...I..." Julie stammered, flushing with embarrassment.

But then Ashe began to turn white. And whiter still. We could see beads of sweat forming on the bald man's round head as his face scrunched up into a demonic twitching grimace.

"What's the matter?" exclaimed Julie.

Now Ashe was vibrating like a guitar string. then he grabbed his side as if an arrow had struck him.

"Call a doctor," I said to Abdul, who instantly lifted a receiver and began to tap numbers.

Grunting in pain, Ashe collapsed to the floor.

"Did I do that?" asked Julie worried.

I shook my head.

I knelt beside the writhing man in black.

"We called 911. An ambulance is on the way," I said. "Do you know what it is?"

Ashe, sweating and grimacing in pain, rolling from side to side, nodded with eyes squinted closed.

"Gallstones," he said.

Chapter 134

With the last flashing light of the ambulance receding down the drive, Abdul, Julie, and I walked to Abdul's Mercedes Benz.

We both sat down in it in complete silence for several seconds.

Finally Abdul started the car and began to drive off.

"What a horrible little man," said Julie.

"Right, and we learned practically nothing," I said.

"Other than about the Big Stomp," said Abdul.

"Yeah, which sums up to: It's not nice to mess with Mother Nature."

"Or she'll stomp you," I said.

But on the ride home, Julie was strangely quiet. I looked at her several times. Each time she avoided my gaze and looked out the side window.

We finally pulled up in front of Julie's apartment, and Abdul's Mercedes lurched to a halt.

Julie prepared to get out of the car without a word.

Then she looked at us and said, "Unfortunately, Ashe is right."

"Oh, Julie, no, not the Big Stomp! It isn't so," corrected Abdul.

"No, not that," said Julie, "the part about me being a little black spider unconsciously waiting in the corner. At least Ashe knew who his mother was. I just had some kind of fantasy that drove me..."

Before I could think of something to say Julie got out and slammed the car door.

She walked so slowly up the steps the long black dress barely swayed.

Chapter 135

Abdul and I had been sitting in the car in silence for several minutes, each thinking his own thoughts.

Then something fell from on high and shattered on the sidewalk beside the car. I looked out on the cement to see small glittering icy shards, and a single wire ring.

It was Julie's monocle.

"Boss, this is too much for her. I think she is in trouble," said Abdul gravely.

Chapter 136

The phone rang at about 9:30 at my home. I pushed the pause button on my Mario-Brothers cart race, freezing the little flying TV images as they flew around an impossible course in Cyberspace.

"Yes?"

"Morgan, were you watching the news?" came back Julie's voice over the ear piece.

"No, I wasn't. Why?"

"The newscast just said Dr. Needler is dead," said Julie breathlessly.

"What happened? A drug overdose?" I asked.

"They just said he was found in his office with a hole in his head."

"Doesn't sound like an experiment you perform on yourself," I said.

"No, it appears someone took a drill and drilled a hole in his skull," said Julie. I could hear her swallowing uneasily.

"It was probably that one used to let the evil spirits out," I said.

"Well, it certainly didn't save his life either," said Julie.

There was a long pause.

"Morgan?" said Julie.

"Yes?" I said.

"I'm scared."

"Well, that's right, Julie," I said. "That's the right thing to be. Someone is calling on the people we investigate. And they're coming up short in the health department. I'm not sure who it is."

"Do you suppose it's the Emperor, covering his tracks?"

"I don't know, whoever it is seems to be behind us, not covering up tracks in front of us..."

"Do you think the Emperor is this gruesome killer?" said Julie. This was a hard concept to think about, that part of her ancestry might be party to real human harm.

"I don't know," I said.

"Oh, Morgan, I don't know if I want to discover all this," said Julie. I could almost see her shaking her blond head in dismay.

"We can only keep going, no matter how miserable the trail," I said.

There was a long silence at the other end of the line.

"And Julie?" I said.

"Yes?"

"Do me a favor tonight, be sure to lock your door."

The receiver clicked off.

Chapter 137

I'd been thinking a lot. Somebody, including us, was after the Emperor. I decided to try forcing somebody's hand.

I picked up the phone and dialed Abdul's number.

"Hello?" came back in Abdul's voice.

"I have a guess who the Emperor is..." I said.

"Boss, don't say anything!" Abdul nearly shouted into the phone.

"I'll be right over to your apartment."

I hung up.

Chapter 138

As I got out of my car, the evening had thrown black blankets over the building sides. Dim street lights sent out grey circles that barely touched the walls.

As I walked toward Abdul's apartment steps, I looked ahead.

There, like a doorman, stood a big hulk of a man. He was dressed in a long raincoat, and for a second I thought it was Sugar Ray Mohamed Ali come to meet me.

But I was wrong. As I stepped up the first steps, I saw it wasn't Sugar Ray. The big man looked down at me with a monstery grimace. I felt he meant me no good. And then I indeed recognized him.

It was Sugar's brother.

"How are you, Sugar Ray Cassias Clay?" I said.

By way of answer, Sugar's brother lifted me by the lapels, growled convincingly in my face, and walked me, my feet tiptoeing the ground, down the stairs and into the alley. Once in the alley blackness, he gave me a shove that launched me airborne.

I thumped into the alley wall with a percussion that set all my innards jangling.

I was just straightening, when Sugar's brother put a left hook into my belly that made me lose my pork chop dinner.

The huge black man stood back in disgust, looking at his hurling victim.

"What do you want?" I said between gasps. I was going to have to have a second or two to recover if I was going to get out of this.

"What do you know about the Emperor?" growled Sugar Ray Cassias Clay.

I straightened.

"Nothing, Mr. Clay," I said.

Then I swung. Unfortunately, it was low and my fist clipped his shoulder before it went up to his jaw.

Sugar Ray blinked off the blow like a tyrannosaurus bopped by a surprise sparrow. Then it bent back to the kill.

"Not again with the lapels," I said as he hoisted me up and tossed me to the other side of the alley. I rolled and hit the side of my head a bad smack.

"Tell me what you know about the Emperor," said Sugar Ray Cassias Clay.

He walked over, bend down, put a squashing hand on my chest, and lifted his huge fist to aim a stiff one at my head.

While he was taking aim, I reached in my jacket. I found my 32 caliber Smith & Wesson and as Sugar Ray Cassias Clay held me down to give me a good pummel, I pulled the gun and fit the muzzle like a key up his right nostril.

"Don't move," I said, "Or I blow your nose."

Chapter 139

Sugar Ray Cassias Clay blinked momentarily in surprise.

"Up!" I said.

The monstery hulk slowly rose, guided by the muzzle of the 32 up his snoz.

"Now. Who do you work for?" I said.

Sugar Ray Cassias Clay stood there, silent as a hooked fish.

"Who do you work for?" I shouted. I clicked back the hammer. When the pistol snapped, the huge black man moved even more uncomfortably.

"Achmyer, John Achmyer," said the deep voice.

I pulled the gun from the monster's face.

I backed up three safe steps.

"I should kill you," I said. "But I won't. You're the brother of Sugar Ray Mohamed Ali, an important source of information of mine, and he'd probably be unhappy if I actually killed his brother."

Sugar Ray nodded begrudgingly.

"Get out of here," I said.

The monster walked from the alley with bowed head.

I decided to go to Abdul's and wash my gun.

Chapter 140

The door opened and Abdul stepped back in silence.

"I gotta wash my gun," I said, and brushed past him.

"What's up, Boss?" said Abdul dogging my steps as I walked into the kitchen, turned on the faucet, and rinsed and dried my 32's muzzle.

"Somebody met me on the way to your apartment," I said.

Abdul moved uneasily from foot to foot. He took in my ruffled and soiled clothes. He then looked nervously at his own door, thankfully chained and locked.

"Who? What happened?" asked Abdul.

I related my alley tussle with Frankenstein's brother. I described the battering, my loss of dinner, and the eventual denouement when I fetched up my piece and caught the monster by the nose.

Abdul expressed the proper amounts of surprise and dismay.

"What did he want?" asked Abdul.

"He wanted, like all of us it seems, to find out who the Emperor is."

"And have you found out? Did you tell him?" asked Abdul. His eyes were trained on me in concern.

"No, I couldn't tell him. I don't know. It was just a Morgan's Eagle-Eye Detective ruse, seeing as how we seemed to be pretty well wirc tapped."

"I can fix that, Boss," said Abdul, "I'll clean for taps tomorrow."

"No, don't. Not just yet. If we know it, it's something we know. You know? We might use it again."

Abdul shrugged that this was a hopeless idea but he would abide it.

"Did you find out who this man worked for?" asked Abdul.

"No," I said.

"Now what?" asked Abdul.

"We watch our backs," I said.

Chapter 141

I was alone in my office. I hadn't told Abdul that John Achmyer had sent a henchman to accost me in the alley. Information was leaking out of my office so fast, I had to keep it back somehow.

The phone rang.

"Hello, Morgan," I said.

"Guten Morgan to you, too," said a deep voice that could only be Sugar Ray Mohamed Ali.

"Sugar Ray," I said, "I met your brother last night. In a dark alley. He almost killed me. That's why I wanted you as a bodyguard."

"Yeah, Morgan, I heard."

"So?" I said.

"So...no hard feelings. I appreciate that you didn't ice him."

"I rarely do that."

"I know, but you could have," said Sugar Ray. "He'd punched you up. It would have been self-defense. Pro-boxer and all. And he's my brother, so I would have had to ice you."

"Sure, sounds right to me," I said.

"So, I owe you this. You're looking for the Emperor."

"Everybody seems to know that," I said.

"Well, you know that brown guy that worked for the Emperor? The one who gave me the money for the job on Sugar Ray Cassias Clay?"

"Yeah?"

"He works for you."

Chapter 142

It took me a moment to digest this.

"Morgan?"

"Yeah, I'm still here."

"He works for you, you get me? He's the one delivered the envelope to me. That's why I said watch your back."

"Why didn't you tell me sooner?" I asked, shaken.

"When I went to your office, he was there. He met me at the door. He told me to take off, and if I talked, the Emperor would be sure to put an ace of spades in my hat band."

"Hmm," I said.

"I got a kid, you know? But since you didn't damage little CC, I owe you."

The monster Sugar Ray Cassias Clay was "little CC" to his brother?

I was struck dumb with information overload.

"That's it," said the voice, and the phone clicked dead.

Chapter 143

I picked up the phone and dialed Abdul's number.

"Hello?" came back in Abdul's voice.

"I have a guess who the Emperor is..." I said.

"Boss, that ploy will not be working twice. You didn't find out anything the first time, only getting good bumps in the process."

"I'm coming over right away," I said. "I'm going to tell you who the Emperor is..."

There was a hesitation on the other end of the line.

"Now, Boss?" said Abdul.

I put down the greatest American detective tool ever invented and hung up.

Chapter 144

I drove over to Abdul's first floor apartment. I'd knocked and stood only a second looking at Abdul's "Extraordinaire" sign, when a nervous looking Abdul appeared in the door.

I walked in and sat down on the near couch.

Abdul shut the door, carefully locking it. Then he turned and said, "Well, Boss, tell me what you know." He smiled affably, rocking on his heels and hunching his shoulders like a kid forced to listen to something he didn't really want to hear.

"You know that bodyguard I wanted to hire, Sugar Ray Mohamed Ali? The one you sent away before visiting Dr. Billie Kookie?" I began.

"Yes, Boss," said Abdul.

"Well, he thinks you work for the Emperor. He said you paid him for a job for the Emperor once."

"No, Boss, that can't be right. I don't work for the Emperor. It's somebody else," said Abdul. Abdul looked at me with pleadingly arched eyebrows.

"That's right, Sugar Ray was wrong. You don't work for the Emperor," I said. Abdul relaxed visibly and nodded.

Then I said it.

"Abdul, you are the Emperor."

Chapter 145

If Abdul were in the dictionary, you would have found him somewhere between flabbergasted and flummoxed.

"Now, don't go giving me any of that 'Oh, Boss, not me' stuff," I said evenly. "I've been shot at, ridden a mule fifteen miles through mountains, attended a hit-and-run party for a Klan member, and punched so hard I lost my lunch. I don't want any more shuffling. I know who the Emperor is, and it's you. This has been one big amazing chase you've led me on, and I want to know why. Now. And you tell me now, or I can just go up to Julie's and tell her, and you can explain it to both of us."

"Wait, wait, Boss," said Abdul.

"I'm not waiting for anything. You've played me for a fool, feeding me the information you wanted, starting with a birth certificate you altered to take Anne Elisabeth initials off. You even handed me the list of suspects, many of whom have come up short in the health department because someone was trailing me as we checked these characters out. I don't see all the connection yet, but I want to see the connections now. I want the story, and the whole story. Because there's someone after you, and I may let them have you."

"Who's after me?" asked Abdul.

"It was Achmyer sent Sugar Ray Cassias Clay to waylay me. I found out from him."

"Achmyer! Okay, okay, Boss. Then we've found out who's been after me, and who contacted Julie. So the investigations over. Okay."

Abdul motioned for me to follow him. He went to a closed door on the side of his apartment. It was metal with a outdoor lock on it. It looked like it might lead to the parking garage. Abdul fished out some keys and busied himself unlocking the door.

Finally he bid me follow him through it.

I walked over and surprisingly entered a large room the size of a bus terminal. It was windowless, but brightly lit, with a vast red carpet covered with multicolored Arab and Berber rugs, Ming vases, tropical plants and palms, a huge pink ceramic fountain trickling with naked cherubim, oriental floor cushions, glass tables, and what looked to be expensive art pieces framed in solid gold frames. It looked like the boudoir of any immensely rich Arab Sheik as I imagined one.

In the middle of the room stood a huge green machine, humming with a beehive of blinking lights and coiled wires here and there, all connected to a dozen or so computer terminals.

I realized I was probably looking at a Cray super computer.

Abdul sat down on one of the cushions and bid me sit as well.

Abdul heaved a sigh.

"Yes. I am the Emperor," said Abdul.

Chapter 146

"Where do I begin?" asked Abdul.

"Try the beginning, how did you become the Emperor?"

"Can I get you some tea or something? This may be a long story," said Abdul helpfully.

"No, I want to hear from the beginning what this has been all about."

Abdul bowed slightly in my direction. He took a deep breath.

"Do you remember when I told you about Roxanna?" asked Abdul. "Well, when Roxanna died, it was doing terrible things inside me. I vowed to never be poor again. So I did as I told you, I returned to Scotland, I studied computers, I became adept at programming. I worked hard, very hard. I'm making good money. One day, I'm getting a job with a company that was developing a money inspection machine, Spinardi Swiss International. They hired me to do programming required to examine the printed sheets of new currency for flaws as it came off the presses. Oh, Boss, it was a big machine, with a lot of complex programming I was doing. Yes."

Abdul shook his head with remembrance.

"You see I was building a computer model of the images of the currency, which the machine would check the newly printed bills against. It was not just a picture of a printed sheet of money, it was a computer model of what was acceptable money. When the computer had this model in its mind, it would look at the bills through CCD's, TV camera's really, and see where the printed sheets didn't match. It took years to develop. But I did well."

"Well, how does that make you a rich man?" I asked.

"Well, Boss, after that I went off on the money making business on my own. You see, Boss, if you can create a computer model of sheets of money for inspection purposes, it is no great shakes to make your computer model print perfect money."

"Counterfeiting?" I said.

"No, Boss, not counterfeiting, printing perfect money. Money that even the Spinardi Swiss Infini-checque machine could inspect and would accept as good bills. No one could tell the difference between my bills, and the government's. No one. I could literally do it for any currency the world over. Wherever a Spinardi Swiss Infini-checque was sold, I had a key into creating unlimited funds."

"I purchased a printing company in a secluded area outside Geneva. I quadrupled the employee's salaries, and posted arm guards. I told them for now on, they would be printing currency for governments on contract, and that they must be sworn to absolute secrecy or risk having criminals or terrorists break in and rob and kill us all. They were to tell anyone inquiring about our work that we printed confidential military specs and corporate securities. We fortified with security guards. Then we started printing. Our product was driven off in trucks they didn't know where."

Abdul tilted his head, "In a short time, I had not millions, but billions at my disposal. I have to admit, I'm thinking I am one clever rascal."

"With Denmark and Belgium going down the economic tubes in the first place."

"Yes, well, I made some initial mistakes. I had to learn to handle immense sums. I have to tell you that after a few months, I was able to put pressure on the world economy to put Denmark and Belgium back in shape.

I didn't leave all those kids pushing wheelbarrows of cash destitute for long."

"And then I had another problem."

"What was that?" I asked.

"Then I was the wealthiest man that'd ever been on Earth," sighed Abdul.

Chapter 147

"So, what did you do then, go out, throw money around, and have all the women you ever wanted?" I asked.

"Oh, no Boss," said Abdul seriously, "I've always had all the women I wanted. Women are going for the gangly type."

Abdul smiled sheepishly.

"No, at first, with immense funds, I recreated my childhood. You know, the huge homes of the British rich? I had one. I purchased an immense mansion, nearly a Taj Mahal, complete with servants and gardeners and cooks and drivers in the hills of Darjeeling, back in India. An immense house, an Alhambra really, with many gardens. Exactly one I'd looked at with wonder when I was so young watching the British rich. I even had one guy whose whole job was to turn the volume up and down on my stereo all day. And I'm filling it with all kinds of things I'm buying. I'm having 10 cars, a racehorse stable, dune buggy, a string of mules, two camels, two small airplanes, an aquarium so big I had an alligator in it. I had a carousel shipped in from California custom-made with only kangaroos as animals. I had a roller coaster with mouse cars. I had radar installed, and artworks from the four corners of the world. I'm having it all in my little Indian home of childhood fantasy. And I'm having exotic parties with Hula dancers at 4:00, and slam dancing at 8:00."

"So, what's so terrible about that?" I asked.

"Oh, well Boss, after a year of that, I'm always seeing my poor Indian brethren, passing them walking on the dirt roads in my Mercedes. I'm seeing them poking a donkey in the rump with a stick, the donkey carrying big haystacks on its back. I'm see raggedy-clothed children with scabby faces and legs." Abdul hesitated a moment.

"I'm having a good time, I'm so rich. But Boss—" Abdul looked at me solemnly.

"The Prince can't dance on the people's severed toes."

Chapter 148

"So I suppose it was about that time that you made your donation to Mother Teresa?" I asked.

"Precisely, Boss, I sent her a small gift. $250 million dollars."

Chapter 149

"So what did you do then?" I asked.

"Oh, I'm changing my ways. I'm investing my money in ways that I think are good. I had so much money! If a company was polluting the Ganges, I bought the company and cleaned the river. If the Colombians were shooting their homeless children, I bought orphanages and made shelters. I'm financing certain politicians, and I'm jailing others. I'm hearing of a border war killing 10,000 Hutus, so I'm buying up all the weapons. I'm exerting my influence in secret ways."

"So I spent much time making timely donations. Placing my money and power where it helps some, and hurt others. After all, Boss, I'm a brown man, I'm not lily white."

"Donations like to Sergeant Voznesensky and Joseph Hateplum?"

Abdul nodded, "Yes. You see, you give certain people money, and they will work to fulfill their visions. And if their visions are poor they become imprisoned in their visions. It works out almost magically. I gave Voznesensky his money, and he builds his own military prison. I give Hateplum money, and his followers get better educated and the hater's vision dies. So I am influencing people, good doers, criminals, in secret ways. And if things go wrong with the criminals, they continue to do hateful things, I can always call the FBI. I am building a huge information network," said Abdul waving backhanded at the Cray super computer blinking behind him, "so that I can keep better tabs on the world."

"And, did you take revenge on those who mocked you as a kid back in Scotland?" I asked.

Abdul laughed and shook his head.

"Oh, well, yes, I was tempted. I was tempted to serve some justice for being untouchable in the British castes. But, in the end I did nothing."

"I didn't want to be a slave to working out my bad feelings."

"You see, basically I was a god. And if you live out your bad feelings, you are a bad god. And if you live out your good feelings, you are a good god."

Chapter 150

"But one day, something happened in my Indian home that is really hitting me," said Abdul.

"A poor addled beggar man is coming into my garden. He is grabbing up a large stone and grabbing my daughter. He's shouting he's going to smash her head if I don't give him food."

"So Roxanna and you had had a child," I said.

"Yes, we are having a baby before Roxanna died. Our poor slow Anna Elisabeth. And in my home, I'm having an old woman who also has a retarded child, nearly the same age as Anna Elisabeth, 17 years old. This woman is taking care of her son and my daughter."

"Would that be Aunty Dotty?" I asked.

Abdul nodded, "Yes, good one, Boss."

"And here this beggar is threatening to harm my daughter. One addled person threatening to harm another addled person. All because he knew I'm having a lot of money," Abdul shook his head and sighed.

"What happened?" I asked.

"Oh, you are knowing Aunty Dotty, she's going up to this beggar man and kicking him in the unmentionables."

Chapter 151

"But then I knew, if people found out about my true wealth, my family would always be in grave danger. And another thing happened."

Abdul looked at me with a half smile.

"Anna Elisabeth became pregnant. She was going to have a baby."

Chapter 152

"Who was the father?" I asked.

"It could only be Aunty Dotty's son. Imagine, a baby born of two poor retarded children. Aunty Dotty's son, oh, he was a good boy. And Anna Elisabeth and he had always been friends. But..."

"But what? Did they get married?"

"No, you see he died. He just stopped living one day. Anna Elisabeth was only three months from having the baby."

"Aunty Dotty's world collapsed. Anna Elisabeth is missing Aunty Dotty's boy, but not understanding. Our worlds are turning upside tippy turvey."

"And so, I'm making plans. I'm bringing my family to the United States to hide my vast wealth and protect my family. I'm taking Aunty Dotty, and Anna Elisabeth, and we're coming to live here. And Anna Elisabeth is having her baby."

"Julie?" I said.

"Yes, and a last unexpected thing happened," said Abdul.

"What was that?" I asked.

"Julie is born normal."

Chapter 153

Well, I admit, I was hearing quite an Indian saga. I realized, like the roots of most plants, Julie's family roots were quite tangled.

"So, I'm setting up my family and hiding my wealth here," continued Abdul. "Are you sure you wouldn't like some tea? I can fix some nearly instantly?"

I waved Abdul off.

"Well, here is Julie, whose mother is handicapped, and whose father was handicapped and died. Whose life is in danger because of me and the money I'm making. I had opened the money window and it seemed it was closing on my family. Oh, Boss, I thought hard on this. What life was this poor baby to have? What foundation would she have thinking her true parents were imbeciles? What would she grow up thinking of herself? Should I give this poor baby away, take Anna Elisabeth's life away from her and Aunty Dotty? You see, Boss, I considered everything. And, I settled for this. I told Aunty Dotty that she should always act as if she had adopted Anna Elisabeth and Julie, her granddaughter. They would live up there." Abdul pointed toward the ceiling and pointed down again, "And I here in the basement."

"So Aunty Dotty, Anna Elisabeth, and Julie are separated from me, so that should anyone find out that I was the Emperor, they at least would be protected. You know, Boss, it's true, if your weekly paycheck will pay a year's salary for a 10,000 man army, somebody is going to mount one and bring it in through your door. I'm not having that hanging over my head and the heads of my family."

"Why didn't you just live with Aunty Dotty and take care of Anna and Julie? You were her grandfather and Aunty Dotty her grandmother."

"Oh, Boss, well, you are knowing Aunty Dotty. Crotchety. I'm just not wanting to be living with her as man and wife."

As one camel's unmentionable to another, I understood.

Chapter 154

"And that picture from Sneakleman?" I asked.

"It is a picture that Anna Elisabeth drew when she was little. I let her play once in a mountain of money," Abdul smiled at the foolishness. "Anna Elisabeth is giving me the picture, bringing it home from school one day. I liked it. I brought it to my Geneva office on a trip. I put it on a bulletin board where Sneakleman sneaked it."

"Aunty Dotty and Anna Elisabeth were doing fine in our new home," sighed Abdul.

I knew there was a "But" to follow.

Chapter 155

Abdul looked at me and continued.

"But little Julie, after years here, she was not doing well. She was four or five, adopted alone in an apartment with only her sister and old Aunty Dotty. Oh, Boss, poor Julie. We could see she was not doing well. Not at all. She was so sad faced. Her spirits hung on her like old clothes. She was not getting what she needed: Momma love. She didn't even know who her mother was! Woe, poor, Julie. She was like a dwindling plant in a window sill. A plant in a flowerpot that you can't make grow. Like your geranium, Boss, that you might knock off with you elbow at any time. Aunty Dotty and I felt helpless to help her."

Abdul shook his head.

"And then I'm thinking. I'm thinking how I can give her hope, give her at least a picture of her mother."

"And so you had that portrait made, of the beautiful woman in the tiara and ball gown, and had it sent to her as her mother," I said.

Abdul reached under a cushion exposing a small black remote control device. He pressed a button and nodded to direct my attention to the near wall.

A big projection of the portrait of Julie's mother magically appeared in a golden frame. I could see it was digitally produced on a hidden screen. But the beauty of the woman, her distant gaze, her deep blue gown, her small but shining tiara burned brightly on the wall before me.

"So you gave her a false portrait of her mother," I said solemnly, knowing how deeply it had affected Julie's life. It had turned her around and oriented her toward success. But also had isolated her from herself.

Unmoving, Abdul gazed profoundly at the image. Finally he shook his head.

"Oh, Boss, it is not entirely a false portrait. You see, that is a picture of Roxanna."

Chapter 156

Abdul turned away and would not look at me.

Chapter 157

"Excuse me, Boss. Some of this is difficult to speak of," said Abdul, facing me again with blurry eyes and weak smile.

I nodded.

"So what started all this trouble?" I said, waving a hand around me in general.

"One day, Anna Elisabeth is sick. And she is coming back from the doctors with a report: She has leukemia. She's needing a bone marrow transplant. The doctor reports Julie is not the right type. We have a dilemma."

"Then, shortly afterwards, that note about the Emperor being Julie's father appears under Julie's door. It means Julie should look for the Emperor, find her real father. But with the two things happening so closely together, I'm growing suspicious. Who knew about this Emperor and Julie, how? I'm checking and have Anna Elisabeth secretly tested again. She doesn't have Leukemia, she is slightly anemic. Someone has falsified the doctors reports, hired this doctor, who is now missing. I realized someone is trying to reach the Emperor. Through Julie."

Abdul swallowed, "It is my worst fear."

"So, I'm getting on my computer. And sure enough, there in the FBI files is the report on Willie the Sneak. It turns out he is one of the Emperor's messengers from Geneva. He has stolen some things from my company, my office. That transfer slip, and a picture from my bulletin board. Willie was putting two and two together. He thinks he has a clue for finding the Emperor."

"So you were after Willie the whole time?" I asked.

"No," said Abdul shaking his head. "It was not so easy. Willie is coming to the United States and I'm guessing is contacting the people on that list. To see if they would buy his information. So I guessed someone on that list was trying to find me, and trying to find me by having Julie try to find me. Perhaps, they felt if Julie looked they could watch and might have more chance of success. The Emperor was more likely to want to meet with the person they thought was his daughter."

"Why not just stop Julie from looking?"

"Once the window is open, even a crack, it's difficult to keep someone from opening it again," said Abdul.

"So you brought Julie to me, and the FBI list, and had me check them out," I said, "Meanwhile you watched to see who was following. What would happen."

Abdul nodded. Then he grimaced.

"I was never intending to let you find me --only find the criminal who was looking for me. I never suspected that without my help you could find anything at all."

"Thanks for the vote of confidence," I said evenly.

Chapter 158

"So why did you have your men off Willie the Sneak?" I said.

"Poor Willie, I didn't send my men to kill him. I sent them to grab him, to find out who he'd sold his information to. Unfortunately, it must have been Achmyer sent his men to kill Willie, to sweep away any tracks leading back to him. After the first shots, my men were shooting to keep you and Willie alive. Achmyer's men must have been shooting to kill Willie, but keep you alive. They wanted you to keep looking for the Emperor."

"What about Tubbman, what's the story there?"

"Oh, I'm having dealings with him as I first set up my network. As you might guess, I'm sending him my code for his Pip-squeak! program. I was the little Inventions of India company that he stole my code from. He took my code, and never sent me a letter back. But he did what I wanted, he made the program immensely popular. Probably 25 million computers run my application these days. I didn't want the money. You see, I'm putting a black box in my code. A back door. And without that black box no one can run the Pip-Squeak! program. Even Tubbman doesn't know what it does. But it allows me to telephone and access the information on any computer running the program. Tubbman helped me expand my information network to 25 million computers."

"And the rest of the list, all people you made donations to?" I said.

Abdul nodded.

"Even Mother Teresa? Why'd we check her out?"

"Just being thorough," said Abdul, "I was waiting to see what would happen."

"We almost got her kidnapped!" I said exasperated.

Abdul shook his head dismissively.

"Oh, Boss, that old lady, she can take care of herself."

Chapter 159

"So Achmyer's it. What are you going to do now?"

"I will have to think about it. Make a plan," said Abdul.

"And what about Julie?" I asked.

"I don't suppose we can close this window again?" said Abdul. He looked at me with the twisted mouth of false hope.

"Nope," I said. "You're going up and tell Julie the whole story right now."

"But, Boss, it will be affecting her greatly," protested Abdul.

"I know," I said. "But she deserves it and needs it."

"This whole plan, it is almost working," said Abdul with resignation. "It's just I'm forgetting one thing."

"What's that?" I asked.

"The slave is always becoming the master. I made you my devoted servant, and now you are telling me what to do," said Abdul.

Chapter 160

"We're all slaves, but you can choose your master," I said.

Chapter 161

Abdul and I went upstairs to Julie's apartment. We found the door kicked in, the place a shambles. Aunty Dotty was unconscious next to the big portrait of Roxanna. Instead of a red dot, she now had a big red bump on the middle of her forehead. Pinned to the front of her dress was a note. The first sentence read:

"We're through fucking around with you, Mister Nosegun."

Chapter 162

"Boss! Where's Julie and Anna Elisabeth?" Abdul ran down the hallway throwing open doors and calling their names. In a few seconds he came back with a huddling Anna Elisabeth, whose face was crumpled and upset.

I put down the note after finishing reading it.

"They've got Julie," I said.

Chapter 163

I dialed 911 and called for an ambulance for Aunty Dotty. Looking about the room, it appeared she'd put up quite a fight. She was still unconscious, but breathing.

Anna Elisabeth was trembling and clinging to the side of Abdul like a frightened shadow. Her mouth was opened slightly, but she made no sounds, her eyes just kept swishing around the corners of the room.

I handed Abdul the note as we waited for the police and ambulance:

MORGAN,

WE'RE THROUGH FUCKING AROUND WITH YOU, MISTER NOSEGUN. WE WANT TO KNOW WHO THE EMPEROR IS. WE HAVE HIS DAUGHTER JULIE. YEAH, WE KNOW IT'S HER. WE'VE BEEN WATCHING YOU. IF YOU WANT TO SEE HER IN ONE PIECE,

WE WANT TO SEE THE EMPEROR. SAY NOTHING TO THE POLICE, OR SHE'S DEAD. WE'LL CONTACT YOU NEXT AT YOUR OFFICE, THE SO-CALLED MORGAN'S EAGLE-EYE DETECTIVE AGENCY. WE'VE STILL GOT DR. NEEDLER'S DRILL. DON'T MAKE US USE IT.

YEAH, ME, ACHMYER.

Chapter 164

Two hours later we left Anna Elisabeth with a neighbor who had been alerted by the sirens and police cars arrival, and left the still unconscious Aunty Dotty in the hospital. They'd done a catscan and found no breaks in the skull, so the ER doctor expected her to come out okay, but with a smarting head. They would hold her for a day or so to observe for concussion.

Abdul and I went back to my office.

We hadn't told a thing to the police. After a few brief words about it, we'd agreed, we weren't limiting ourselves to legal plans of action.

More precisely, Abdul had fumed, "If I can, I'll be roasting that little laddy's ass over slow hickory."

The Emperor was ticked.

Chapter 165

I shut the office door. Abdul went and sat at his rainbow-striped computer terminal.

"Now we wait. I'm sure they'll contact us soon. Then we'll see what the deal is."

Abdul nodded, uncharacteristically without reply. He chewed his lip a few seconds. Then he began punching keys furiously at his terminal.

I didn't know what he was up to, but at least he was busy.

I picked up the phone and said into the dial tone, "We're here."

A hour later the phone rang.

"Hello, Morgan," I said.

"Well, Mister Detective, nice to talk with you again." I recognized Achmyer's unctuous voice. "I wish you would have called me when you found out who the Emperor was. We wouldn't have had to go to all that trouble, beaning the old lady and such. Grabbing Julie here."

"What do you want done? Let's skip the crap," I said.

"Morgan, I want to know who the Emperor is, and I want a cut of the Emperor's bucks. You know the first, and I can rouse the forces to make the second happen. But nobody has to get hurt here. This is just money talking. Right?" said Achmyer.

"Right," I said. "I remember: hit you on the head with a gold bar and you'd like it."

Achmyer laughed evily. "You got it."

"So what's the deal?" I asked.

"We'll come down there and you tell me who the Emperor is. Then we'll see about returning Julie to you."

"No. I get something in return. You come down here, but you bring Julie, so I can see she's all right. Then we'll make arrangements for her release."

"No, we don't show off the merchandise," said Achmyer.

"Yes. Or, I contact the Emperor, tell him everything, including who you are, and he kills everyone in your building and everyone ever associated with you, and your pets."

Achmyer laughed. "I love a good threat. I'll remember that one."

"Deal?" I said.

"Okay, okay," said Achmyer, "We'll come over at six. Contact the Emperor, if you like. But no tricks, or Julie's in a big hurt. Tell him we just want to do business. We don't want to kill anybody prematurely. People like Julie that is. Tell him as an act of good faith we want a million dollars."

"What if he can't raise the money in that short a time?" I said.

Achmyer bellowed with laughter. "Don't underestimate the wealth of the Emperor. Remember, I've had dealings with him. If he wants to put a million dollars on your table in an hour he can. Tell him, we want it in gold. None of his funny money."

I looked at Abdul and whispered, "He wants a million dollars in gold."

Abdul shrugged, "That's only about 10 twenty-pound ingots. No problem."

I spoke back into the receiver. "Okay, a million bucks in gold. You bring in Julie. Then I tell you who the Emperor is."

"Great," said Achmyer. "It's a date. We'll be there at six. Have the gold there, and the Emperor's real name. We get that, we'll leave Julie."

The phone clicked dead.

Chapter 166

"He's bringing in Julie here at six. He wants to know who the Emperor is. He doesn't seem to really want Julie, or he wouldn't bring her here. He wants a million in gold, too. Can you really do that?" I asked Abdul.

"Sure. I keep a little bit of gold back in my apartment. I'm making custom circuits and wiring connectors with it for the Cray."

"Go get it," I said.

Chapter 167

After Abdul left, I made a phone call to my favorite body guard.

"Sugar Ray Mohamed Ali?" I said into the phone.

"Yes, Morgan, what you need, dude?" said Sugar Ray.

"I've got something heavy going down in an hour at my office. Can you come down?" I asked.

"What's up? Guns?" asked Sugar Ray Mohamed Ali.

"No, an exchange of goods, we just need some muscle behind us for respect."

"Who's paying?" asked Sugar.

"The Emperor."

"Be there," said the monster's voice.

The phone went dead.

Chapter 168

A half-hour later, Abdul had returned, and with ten trips up and down the stairs lugging ingots, we had a stack of gold bars piled on my desk.

"That's a million bucks?" I said, seeing the small size of the stack.

"Now you're getting used to big numbers," said Abdul.

"How do you want to play this?" asked Abdul.

"I'm going to give him the gold, and tell him your name, and get Julie back. That's it. That's what Achmyer wants, and that's all we're going to do. We want Julie back. Once Achmyer finds out who the Emperor is, that's a different problem. If all Achmyer wants is money, you can drown him in it, or hit him over the head with it, for all I care. The Emperor will have to figure a way to finish all this himself. I don't want to know what you plan to do about it. But we're not screwing around where Julie is concerned."

Abdul made a slow nod.

"Agreed," he said solemnly, "We get Julie. Then the Emperor ends all this."

Chapter 169

A half hour later, a big hulking shape knocked at my office door. Abdul looked at me, and I nodded for him to open it.

Sugar Ray Mohamed Ali stepped through the door. He had to duck his head just the slightest to come in.

He looked at me, Abdul, and then the pile of gold.

Without a word, he stepped around behind the pile of gold and just stood there.

Chapter 170

Abdul leaned out the window, then called back, "They're here."

I walked over and looked out my window, careful not to knock the geranium pot off the sill.

A big black limousine was pulling to the curb in front of our building. A door opened, and out stepped the little nazi security guard I'd seen on my first visit to Achmyer's. Inside the car door I saw a woman's leg and ankle. It could only be Julie. On the far side of the car, across the polished roof, I saw a big man stand up, and stand up, and stand up. This was one big dude. I recognized him.

"Sugar Ray Cassias Clay," I said. I looked back over my shoulder at Sugar Ray Mohamed Ali to see if he had any problem with that. Our Sugar Ray merely shook his head.

A man with a bowling ball for a head popped up from inside the car. He looked up to catch me watching from our window.

"Morgan!" he called, "We'll be right up. Let me get Julie safely out of the car here."

At that the security nazi reached in and jerked Julie out of the car by the elbow. Julie nearly stumbled out with the sharp pull.

She stood up frowning, looking around a bit ruffled and worse for wear. There were streaks of mascara under her eyes from her struggles. Her hair had a bird nest in it. The sleeve of her blouse was torn. I was about to shout down to her when the security nazi tugged her quickly into the building.

Sugar Ray Cassias Clay and the squat Achmyer, dressed in prim black suit, followed. I noticed two other cars had come up and parked at the curb, but noone got out. Achmyer had brought some backup.

I withdrew back into my office.

"Here they come," I said.

Chapter 171

There was a bit of discussion outside the blurry window of my office door.

"It's open," I called.

The door pushed in slowly and Sugar's Ray hulking brother stepped in, looking around carefully. His hand was under his jacket, but no gun in sight. After he saw me, then Abdul, he noticed Sugar standing guard by the gold. He blinked.

Then the two black giants stared sternly at each other like prize-fighters facing off for a ten-round fight.

"Sugar," said Sugar Ray Cassias Clay with a guarded nod.

"How's the nose, CC?" asked our Sugar from beside the gold.

Little CC frowned, "Now, don't you go making fun a me, you lame ass, som-bitch."

"I'll make funa you, and knock you loop-da-loop with one left I feel like it," spat Sugar.

"Boys, boys, now no squabbling here," I said.

"Exactly," said Achmyer as he pushed into the room. He held a small black Berreta in his hand, which he waved at each of us as he entered as if

232

casting a spell to catch our attention. He then stepped aside; Julie was pushed through the door. The small security guard, uniformed as usual, entered behind her, sneering. He had a small nickel-plated revolver in his grip.

"Julie, you all right?" I called.

Julie looked around the office from me to Abdul, then with uncertainty at Sugar. Finally she looked back at me and nodded. Her face looked worried and crumpled.

"Don't worry, Julie. This is almost over," I said.

"Right!" jumped in Achmyer cheerfully. "I see you have a shining little pile of gold there for me. Is that really a million dollars worth? It's such a small pile?"

"It's over a million," said Abdul, "It's $400 a troy ounce, that makes about $128,000 per twenty-pound bar, ten bars, a million two-hundred and eighty thousand."

"I certainly like your multiplication there, my little fellow," said Achmyer.

"We've brought the money. All we want is Julie. No funny business, no surprises, nothing. Just take it and leave," I said.

"Oh, now, we've forgotten one little thing," said Achmyer, turning his gun in the air as if twisting a faucet.

"We also want to know who the Emperor is."

"No problem," I said.

Julie straighten up and looked at me with a questioning look.

"That's him, that's your Emperor," I said, pointing directly at the chest of my office-slave.

Looking a bit dour, Abdul waved a finger in acknowledgment.

Chapter 172

"No way!" shouted Achmyer. "You're not pulling any funny business on us! You can't tell me your cockamamie office clerk is the Emperor and expect me to buy it!" Achmyer pointed his gun directly at my nose.

Julie was staring at Abdul who'd been watching her with a pleading look.

Then Julie fainted.

Chapter 173

The little security guard caught Julie against him, holding her up with some difficulty. Achmyer gave him a nod. The guard handed his gun to Sugar's brother, and then produced a knife with a thin evil blade. He put the blade up to the side of Julie's head.

"Listen, you ass, Morgan of Morgan's Eagle-eye Detective Agency," said Achmyer with venom, "You're going to tell us who the Emperor is, or Julie here gets hurt."

"I just told you," I said.

Achmyer shook his head angrily, approached me, and put the muzzle of his Berreta against my chest.

"Tell us who the Emperor is, or we cut her ear off!"

Those were the wrong words.

"Oh, oh," murmured Abdul.

Chapter 174

I pushed over my desk and pulled off a leg.

Achmyer had stepped back surprised.

The little nazi was wide-eyed. Even Sugar's brother stepped back a cautious step.

As the Wrath of God overtook me, Abdul jumped forward and pulled Achmyer's gun toward himself. There was a muffled bump, and I realized Abdul had been shot.

I whacked the little nazi a good one on the pate. It send him down for the count, and I didn't care if he ever got up.

Julie fell in a tangled heap with him.

Sugar jumped forward and planted an excellent right cross on his brother's chin. His brother murmured, "Ah, Sugar" as he twisted and lost consciousness.

I turned to Achmyer. Whatever Achmyer saw in my face, it made him drop his gun and scurry over the heaped bodies and out my door. As I heard his foot steps beating down my stairs, I turned to find Abdul leaning against my desk. He had a blood spot forming on his back.

"Don't let him get away," grimaced Abdul.

I went over to my window. I counted three seconds.

Then I nudged the flowerpot off the sill.

Chapter 175

Achmyer never knew what hit him.

Dazed with dirt in his hair, he fell on his face.

Chapter 176

I was gazing down on Achmyer heaped on the sidewalk, several of his men already jumping from their cars to his aid, when I felt the presence of Abdul come staggering to the window beside me.

I looked over just in time to see him heave a gold ingot out.

Aghast, I looked back down to the sidewalk in time to see the gold bar smash onto Achmyer's head.

He'd never get the chance to tell me if he liked it or not.

Chapter 177

Abdul then slumped to the floor beside me. I quickly knelt to appraise his wound. It was a terrible hole just below his heart. Blood was spilling from it too fast.

"Boss," gasped Abdul.

"Yes," I said.

"Tell Julie, for me? The Emperor was always loving her?"

"Yes," I said.

"Boss," gasped Abdul, trying to pull his focus together on me. "On the computer," and Abdul raised his eyes to his rainbow-striped computer terminal for me to follow, "Will you do something for me?"

"Sure," I said.

"Type 'the window is closed,' okay?" he said.

"Okay, what does that mean?" I asked.

"Just type it," grunted Abdul. "Thanks, Boss."

And Abdul died.

Chapter 178

I called the police and an ambulance. Sugar Ray dragged his brother downstairs and safely away. Julie was just coming around.

I went over to Abdul's computer terminal and typed: The window is closed.

As soon as I typed it, the machine began to buzz and whir and throw fast-fading graphics all over the screen.

I walked over to Julie, knelt, and held her hand.

Chapter 179

The police arrived and it was a pandemonium of notepads and scratching pencils.

Achmyer, a prominent financial leader, was dead. The little security nazi was dead. Abdul was dead. I was taken away in hand-cuffs for safe keeping until everything got sorted out. Julie was walked out the door under the wing of a policewoman guiding her to a cruiser.

Chapter 180

A day later, after all the ruckus with the police had quieted down, I went over to Julie's. She let me into the apartment with a waxen face. Her clothes hung on her lifeless like a wet towel.

Aunty Dotty was still in the hospital, and Anna Elisabeth was doing wash down the hall.

Julie and I sat on the plum couch under the great portrait of the beautiful woman in the blue ball gown and tiara.

I told her the story of Abdul Dallah. And the story of Roxanna. And the story of her real mother and father. I told her how Abdul had had good intentions as he tried to protect his family. Julie slumped a bit more finding her father was also retarded. I finally pointed at the picture and told her that the portrait was not of her mother, but was of her grandmother, Roxanna. It was a portrait of where Julie really came from, her true past, after all.

"Morgan, don't you feel a fool?" Julie asked me. "I mean, you were like me. We ran around in a world made by the Emperor, not really seeing the real world around us the whole time. We did our work, ran our pleasures out, built images of ourselves, me the said psychological archaeologist, ha! and you the sure-footed snuffling detective."

"Snuffling?" I said, "No one's used the word snuffling for me before..."

"You know what I mean. We both were blind, living in the world the Emperor imposed on us."

I shook my head, "Imposed seems a harsh word."

"Imposed," said Julie sternly, "is the word. Morgan, what was my world? A puppet play, a dance of shadows? I didn't know who I was, where I lived, other than what I'd inherited. I didn't even know I needed to go beyond it, beyond what Destiny had handed me. You, the detective, the finder of the lost, you didn't even know who you worked with."

"I didn't," I conceded.

"Doesn't it just make you feel... a complete fool? It does me," said Julie. "I didn't know or understand the loved ones around me. I didn't see my real self. I inherited the handicapped and blurred visions of my ancestry and history. The cruel accidents of family. And I had a fantasy vision that I was carrying around. And what has it led to? Here, my world is in shambles."

"Julie, I am a fool," I said, "I start out a fool, not knowing the answers, on each case I take. I go out asking the questions, and sometimes I find the answers, good or bad. And if I find the thing I'm looking for, I know I found it. And after I find it, it's a different world."

"I can't go back to that old world, with my fantasy family, my fantasy PH. D., my fantasy hopes and projects," said Julie, "Look there is Anna Elisabeth, doing the wash. Eternally doing her wash. Well, the wash, it isn't enough for me. What am I to do now?"

"I find a new case, and begin looking around in a new world. I find a case to serve, to give my heart to, and I serve it, and master it if I can," I said. "Snuffle, snort, shout, or shoot," I said, "I do it with my whole heart."

"That's probably why Abdul loved you," said Julie, looking away from me.

"But I'm not sure he loved me," she said. "He wouldn't have let me live in this box." Julie cast a look about her at the apartment, stopping her gaze for one instant on the picture of her grandmother and her tiara.

"He did," I said. "You can't look at it that way. We all inherit our destiny from the false visions of the past. The people who named you when you were born. You have to put your own window on it."

Julie nodded, but didn't say a word.

She asked me to leave.

I left.

Chapter 181

Many of us grow up living in the cold. It's what we know best how to do. When we have a choice, we sometimes chose to be there, in the cold, because it's what we've always known how to do.

But I knew Julie would want to talk with me further sometime. She just needed a little time for some processing. Like Aunty Dotty says, "The sun and the moon always come out."

Chapter 182

The next day, in my office, I received an envelop addressed to me:

Morgan Theodore Roosevelt Einstein Hercules

Morgan's Eagle-Eye Detective Agency.

1000 Mission Ave Suite #10

San Francisco, CA 97001

I opened the letter and read:

Dear Boss:

If you are receiving this, it is because I am not making it through our adventure. I'm thinking maybe it is best this way.

Please go to my computer immediately and type 'The window is closed' if you have not done so already. I'm making big arrangements, and this will set them in motion. First, the Emperor's money operation will cease, and my little printing company in Geneva will close its doors. All employees will be let go with bountiful severance pay packages that they can retire on. All the Emperor's funds will be disbursed electronically to deserving charities world-wide. All records of the Emperor's existence will be erased. A computer virus will be released that contacts the 25 million computers of my information network and erases the backdoor to the Pip-squeak program. My information network will be closed for good. A team will arrive and dismantle my wonderful Cray computer, and no traces of my works will be left in the building. I have left in tact several investments that I owned legitimately before becoming the Emperor which will provide Julie, Anna Elisabeth, and Aunty Dotty with a decent income for the rest of their lives. No one will be able to recapture the Emperor's wealth or money making power again. This is for the best, Boss. I'm making all arrangements.

Boss, I'm wanting to thank you for all your help. I'm always enjoying working with you to find the lost children.

Your Sincere Office Clerk,

Abdul Dallah

Aka: The Emperor

Aka: The Slave of God

Chapter 183

I went to my office window and looked out over the city, this city of angels, citizens, criminals, and bums for a long time. Lot's of people. But damn few Emperors.

Epilogue One

The next day in the mail, I received an invitation to attend the funeral of one Abdul Dallah. Funeral services would be held at 9 at the Mission Delores.

The phone rang. It was Julie.

"Morgan?" said Julie.

"Hello," I said.

"Morgan, I just received the invitation to the funeral for Abdul," Julie hesitated. "Ah, thank you for making these arrangements. I've been so upset, I didn't even think..."

"No, Julie," I interrupted, "It wasn't me who set up the funeral. I think Abdul had these arrangements all set up himself."

"So, you think he thought he was going to die?" asked Julie.

"I think so," I said.

There was a long pause.

"Julie," I said.

"Yes, Morgan?"

"Can I pick you up for the funeral tomorrow?" I asked.

"Yes, please. If you would," said Julie.

We set a time.

I hung up feeling no better.

Epilogue Two

I drove over to Julie's to pick her up for the funeral. As I entered the building I saw the whitened and empty square on the wall where Abdul's Concierge Extraordinaire sign had hung.

I was looking at the missing sign when I heard commotion in the stairwell. I looked up to see Julie, dressed in a high-shouldered black dress, descending the stairs followed by Anna Elisabeth and Aunty Dotty. All wore black dresses. Aunty Dotty was also wearing the white helmet of a head bandage. She'd placed an angry red dot on the bandage where her normal forehead mark should have been.

"Morning," I said.

"Morning," said Julie. Disappointingly, she said nothing more. Anna Elisabeth smiled. Aunty Dotty frowned and said nothing.

I ushered the three into my little car.

Ten minutes later, without a word between us, we'd crossed the city, up Market, and were about to turn onto Delores, when I found my route to the Spanish mission blocked off by a barricade and police motioning us around the block.

I drove down a side street as close to the Mission as I could, luckily finding a vacant parking place blocks farther down by the park.

As we got out of the car, we were surrounded by hundreds of milling people flooding the streets and park.

Julie, Anna Elisabeth, Aunty Dotty, and I stood looking around at the throng for a moment. The entire Delores park was filled with people attending some sort of celebration, with booths giving out wine and food samples, soft drinks, pretzel vendors, waiters porting trays of hot hor d'oeuvres, a man dressed in ape-suit juggling bananas, a high stilt-walker dressed in black, a jazz band playing on a small stage up on the hill, people toasting glasses and laughing, and even a Mariachi band, in full Spanish regalia and sombreros, walking and toottling among the crowd. On the far hillside, up a grassy knoll, was strung a large banner between trees:

Bon Voyage, Abdul!

"What do you make of that?" I asked.

Julie shook her head, "Do you think Abdul planned a wake?"

"Well, he was capable of about anything," I said.

We dodged and needled our way through the crowd, heading around the corner toward Mission Delores. As the old church came in sight, I saw this street too was entirely flooded with lines of black cars and dark clothed men and women. It looked like the staging area of a parade.

Julie and I looked at each other with wonder as we pushed our way through the crowd toward the church.

On arriving at the front steps, an old man in black suit with yellow rose boutonniere, holding pictures in his hand, spotted us and signaled to come up the steps.

"We've been waiting for you," said the old man with the flower warmly. I looked and saw the pictures were of Julie, Anna Elisabeth, Aunty Dotty, and myself. Three black-suited men took my three women companions by the arms and escorted them into the church. I followed a close step behind.

Once through the church doors, I saw the pews of the old sanctuary were packed shoulder to shoulder. At the front of a church stood a highly polished closed casket, surrounded by many open peacock tails of bright flowers. Over the coffin was draped a banner that read: "From Slave to Master!" Behind the casket was a priest I recognized standing silently, robed entirely in pink satin.

Dr. Billie Kookie!

Julie and our party were escorted down the center aisle to the first pew which was empty and waiting. Anna Elisabeth, Aunty Dotty, and Julie were seated, then I took a seat next to Julie. I sat and craned my neck to look around.

"Who are all these people?" whispered Julie with wonder.

I looked and there in the back corner, in dark military uniform, was Sergeant Voznesensky, looking suspiciously over the crowd. Two rows in front of him, slumping a bit despondently, sat Bill Tubbman former head of Delco Software. I saw the San Francisco Mayor, Police Chief, and Fire Chief in one pew. I saw a TV star or two I knew in another. And in the far back corner, looking especially nervous as he surveyed the crowd, scowled the bald and unhappy Charles Ashe. He looked ready to run from the room at any second.

Julie waved to several families on the far side of the church. "Most of the apartment house is here, how nice," Julie whispered.

"Looks like it's about everybody," I said.

"How did Abdul do this?" asked Julie.

"He had his ways," I shrugged. "I'm sure everyone received special invitations. Some of which could not be refused."

Dr. Billie Kookie raised his hands and the whole church fell silent.

"We're gathered here today to grieve the passing of a great contributor," Kookie shouted as he began the service. "A contributor to my world, and your world, Yahweh World, and the worlds of many!"

All round the church people spontaneously shouted, "Amen!"

For several minutes, I saw Julie sit dumbfounded.

Epilogue Three

It was a boisterous crowd for a funeral. As Kookie spoke, people were shouting things like "Praise the Lord and thanks, Abdul!", "Thank you! We'll miss you!", and "Hallaeuia, Abdul!"

Dr. Bill Kookie was half-way through his eulogy, having just shouted that God drives a Ford, when a general commotion started up in the back of the church. All heads turned to see what was happening.

In the open door way, an old woman stood dressed in a white robe and white head cloth with blue stripe, tottering down the center aisle toward the alter. She walked toward us, pinching a single white rose in her fingers. She walked with the calm steady steps of someone long used to attending funerals. A general whispering rippled through the crowd.

"Mother Teresa! Mother Teresa!" people breathed all around the church.

The old woman made her way up to the casket and placed her white rose upon its polished surface. She patted the coffin thrice.

Then the old woman came over to our pew, nodded to me, and had me scooch over a bit so she could sit down.

Epilogue Four

Before Bill Kookie finished his eulogy, he raised his hands for silence. The crowd hushed.

"Today, a sad day, when we gather to mourn the passing of Abdul Dallah, I want to take a moment to turn the focus on myself. You see, many of us didn't know Abdul Dallah well, and I didn't know Abdul well. I didn't realize it, but I recently had my first chance to speak with him last week. I didn't even realize it was him. He was, however, an anonymous contributor to each of us. One of the great anonymous contributors."

"Amen!" shouted the Mayor of San Francisco. All heads turned toward him, and red faced with the discharge of one more political secret, the Mayor shrugged good naturedly.

"I want to tell you about something that changed me," shouted Kookie, "You see, dear mourners, I was once a very unhappy man. I was a great minister, I was taking in great deals of money, for the church, and for myself. But more importantly for myself. You see, I was something of a money-grubber. I was, in effect a poor man determined to serve himself of your money."

The whole church was rapt. Many eyebrows were up. Many were not.

Kookie smiled and raised his hands in appeasement.

"But you see, way back around 1987, something happened that changed all that. You see, I received a contribution that I would never forget."

Kookie reached into his robe sleeve and withdrew a small piece of paper and waved it like a signal hanky over his head.

"Brothers, I received an envelope with this note. And in the envelope, I received a check for $250 million dollars."

"Ahhhh," said the crowd collectively.

Julie was frowning.

Billie raised his hands for quiet, "And the note said: 'I was a slave, but I chose you for my Master.'"

"Yours faithfully, Abdul Dallah, Concierge."

Dr. Billie Kookie looked out on the crowd. He smiled with pain and time-worn acceptance.

He repeated slowly, "I was a slave, but I chose you for my Master."

The old mission now filled with a midnight silence.

"And that day, I was a changed man. That day I began building Yahweh World. Yes. It was the start of new things."

"Yeah, Brother!" shouted someone.

"But it wasn't the money that changed me, as you might think. No," said Kookie shaking his head. "You see, it was the little note. The note that said, I was a slave, but I chose you as my Master."

"He chose me as Master," said the priest, and a gleam formed in Kookie's eyes that dropped as a tear.

"It made me think. It made me want to do a little better. It made me want to stop serving myself. And from that day, I didn't worry about money any more. I decided to build Yahweh world, for you, for me, for Abdul, for all of us. You see, from that day on, I wasn't a poor man calling out for money. I was a rich man. I'd heard the call of Abdul Dallah, the call of my people, my congregation and community. I was a rich man with all of you around."

"Say it, Brother!" shouted the San Francisco Police chief.

"I started to have fun. I started to enjoy my life. And I started to enjoy building my church. And, before I knew, yes, I was happy."

Kookie raised the note high over his head.

"Because of a simple note that Abdul Dallah sent me. A note that said, 'I was a slave, but I chose you as my Master.'"

Kookie drew a deep breath.

"And so, today, with all of you who were touched by Abdul Dallah in so many secret ways, let us not mourn his passing. Let us celebrate the passing of a loving slave, and loving master who has lived among us."

With the crowd shouting out its approval and clapping as Kookie praised the inhabitant of the coffin next to him, Julie reached over and took my hand in hers.

She squeezed my hand hard.

We sat together holding hands for the rest of the service.

I hoped this was the beginning of a long relationship.

Then laughing, Kookie invited us all to Yahweh World.

"Because in the words of my favorite poet, Howard McCord," shouted Kookie, "We are a carnival for the lord!"

Julie wept a bit then, and I put my arm around her.

"Good-bye Abdul!" roared the priest, raising his arms with glee.

Dr. Billie Kookie wound up his sermon with a resounding three cheers.

With the rest of the church, Julie and I stood and clapped.

Epilogue Five

For the past five years, Julie has been helping me in my office. As a psychological archaeologist, she's just as good as Abdul at solving the lost children cases. I hope I never have to do without her. Yes, in more ways than one.

We're currently working on the Jesus Gonzales case. He's a kid who seemed to always want to carry around other people's crosses.

Epilogue Six

Every year, on the day of the Emperor's death, I receive at my office a little special delivery.

A pot of geraniums blooming fiercely.

Epilogue Fini

I, Morgan Theodore Roosevelt Einstein Hercules, of Morgan's Eagle-eye Detective Agency, place the pot on my window sill.

Ever ready.